JAKE MADDOX
GRAPHIC NOVELS

HALF-PIPE PANIC

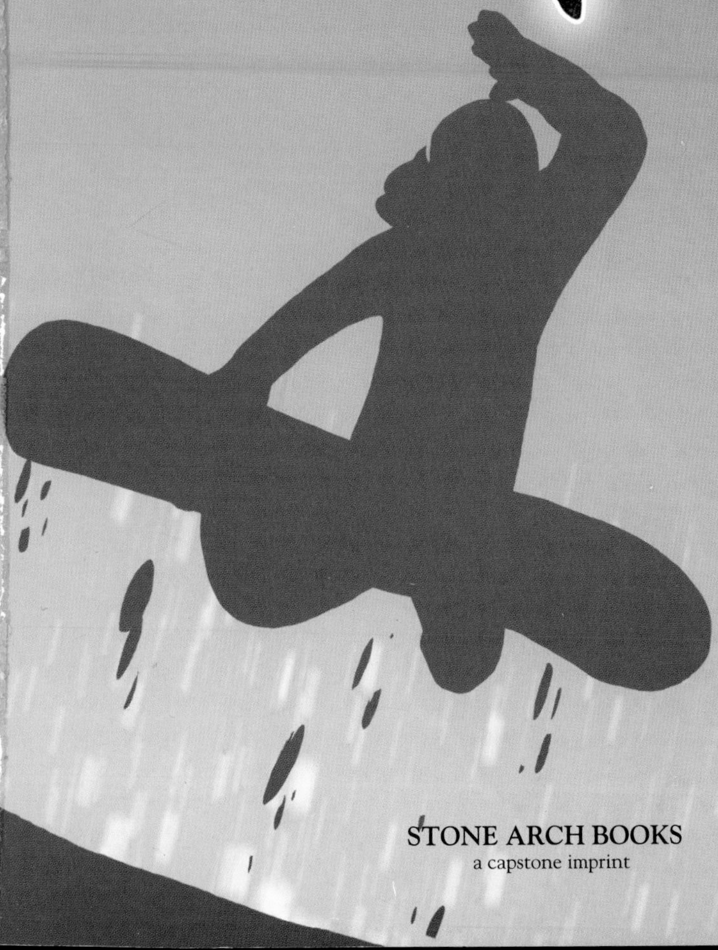

STONE ARCH BOOKS
a capstone imprint

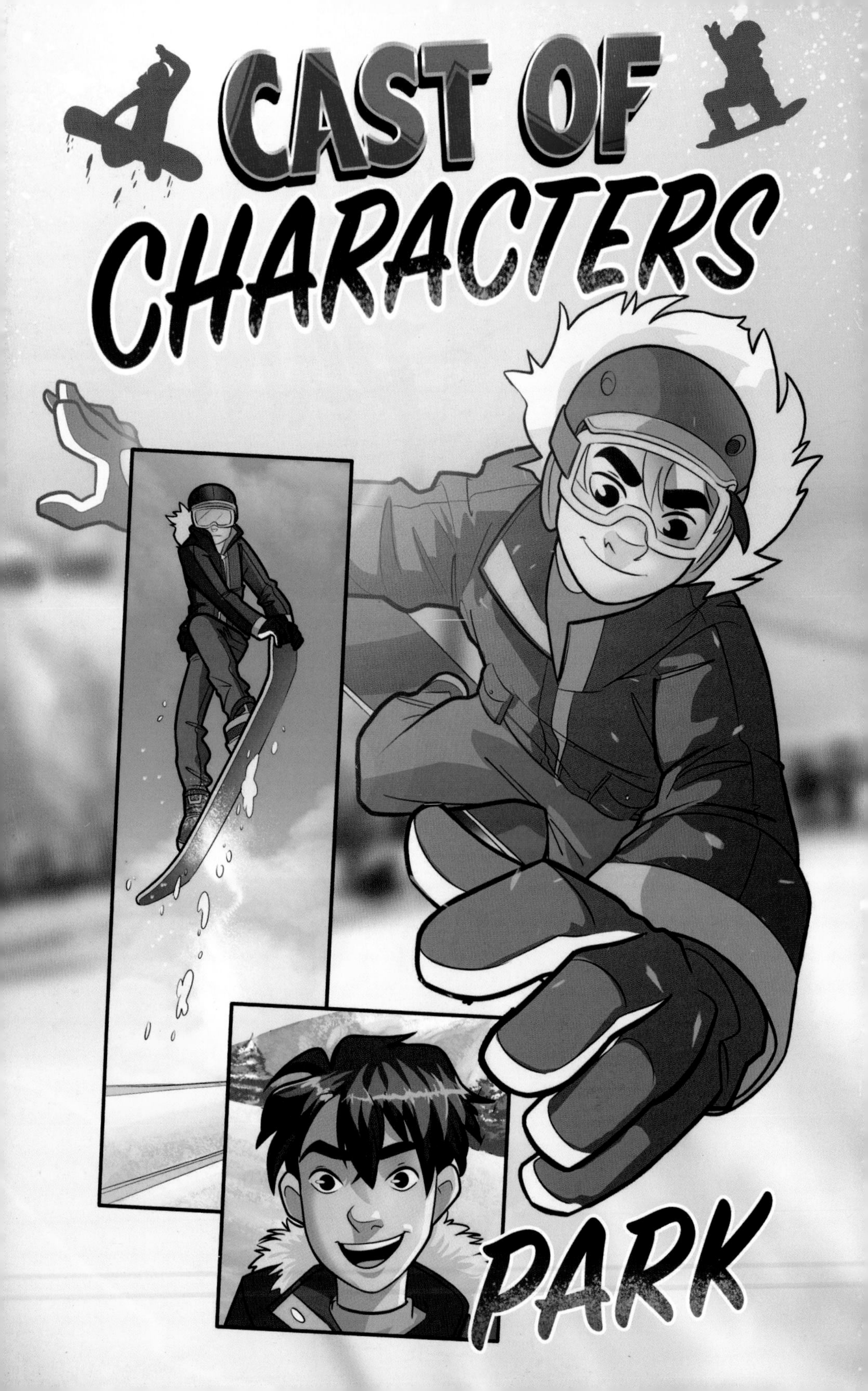
CAST OF CHARACTERS
PARK

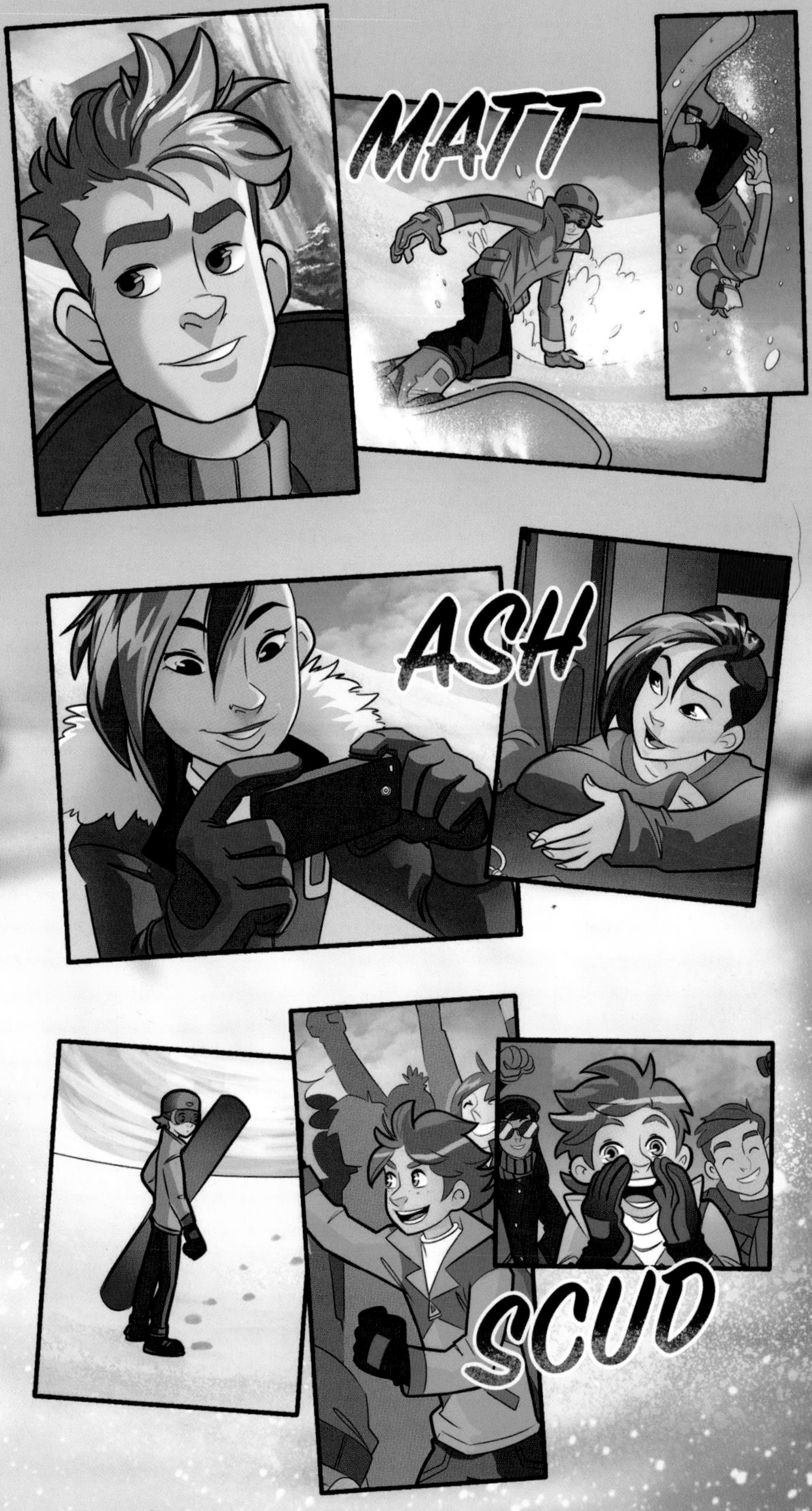
MATT
ASH
SCUD

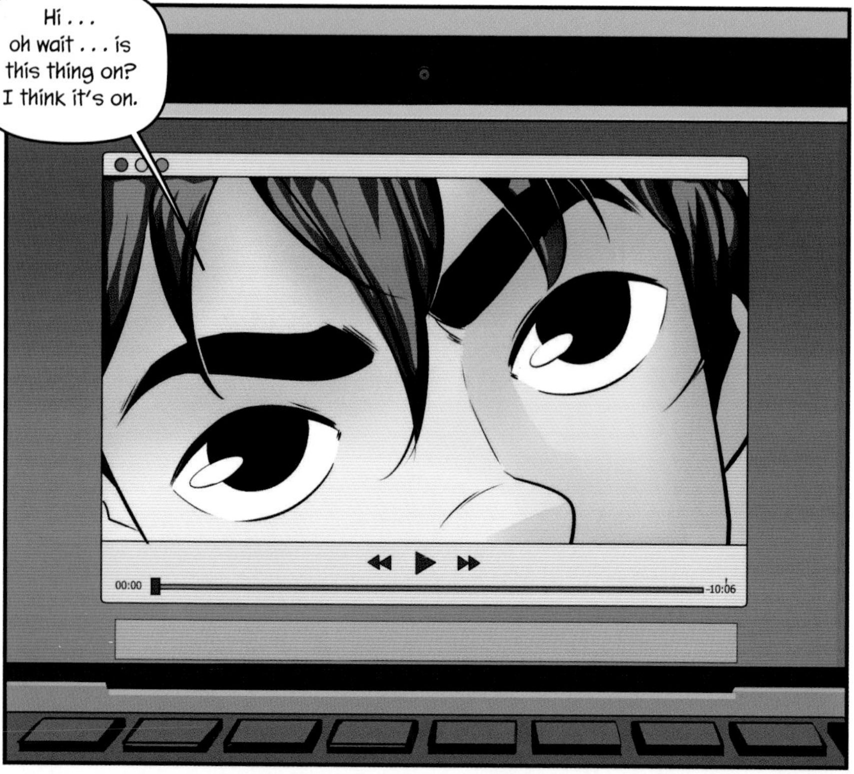
Hi . . . oh wait . . . is this thing on? I think it's on.
00:00
-10:06

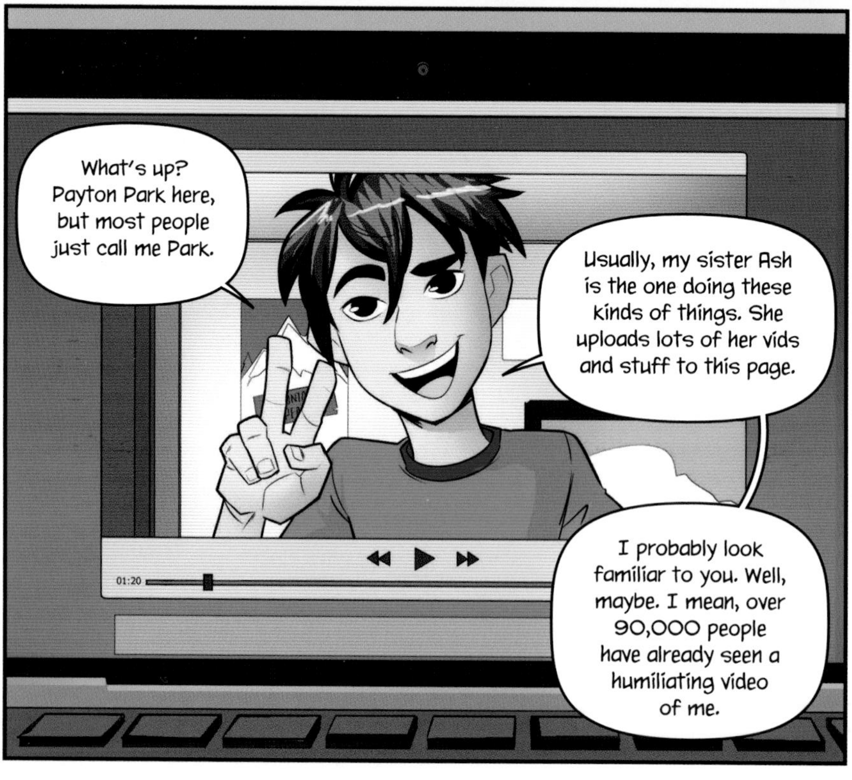
What's up? Payton Park here, but most people just call me Park.
Usually, my sister Ash is the one doing these kinds of things. She uploads lots of her vids and stuff to this page.
I probably look familiar to you. Well, maybe. I mean, over 90,000 people have already seen a humiliating video of me.
01:20

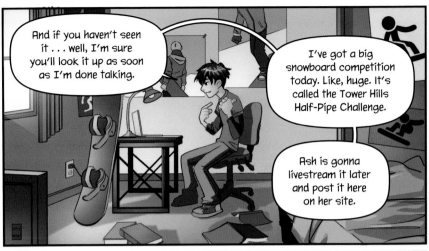

And if you haven't seen it . . . well, I'm sure you'll look it up as soon as I'm done talking.

I've got a big snowboard competition today. Like, huge. It's called the Tower Hills Half-Pipe Challenge.

Ash is gonna livestream it later and post it here on her site.

But I wanted to tell you about what's happened leading up to the competition. Because I've learned a lot.

About having pride, and determination. About friends . . . and fear.

So yeah, let's see. It all started in the same place that it'll end later today.

Out at the half-pipe at Tower Hills . . .

03:20   -10:06

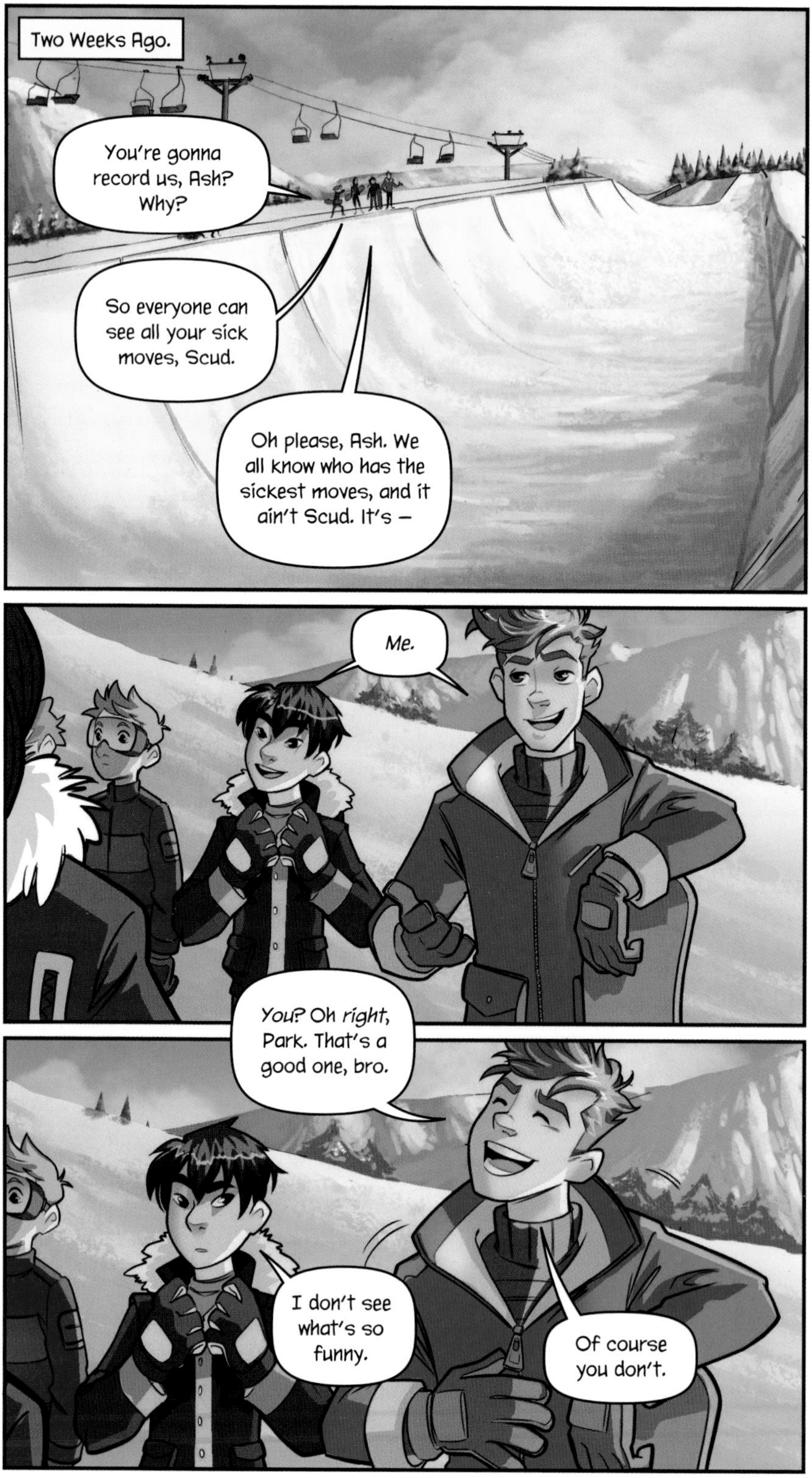
Two Weeks Ago.
You're gonna record us, Ash? Why?
So everyone can see all your sick moves, Scud.
Oh please, Ash. We all know who has the sickest moves, and it ain't Scud. It's –
Me.
You? Oh right, Park. That's a good one, bro.
I don't see what's so funny.
Of course you don't.

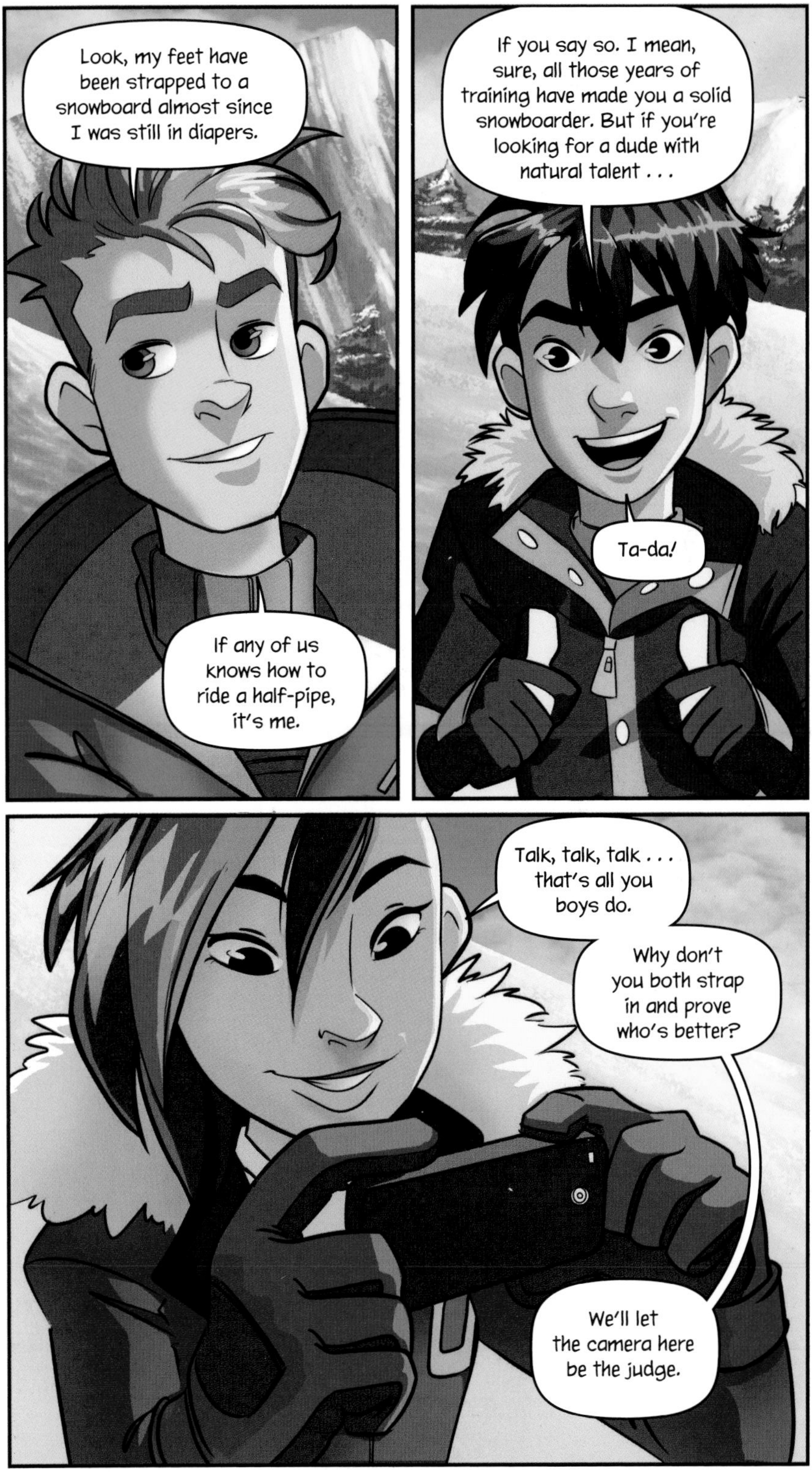
Look, my feet have been strapped to a snowboard almost since I was still in diapers.
If any of us knows how to ride a half-pipe, it's me.
If you say so. I mean, sure, all those years of training have made you a solid snowboarder. But if you're looking for a dude with natural talent . . .
Ta-da!
Talk, talk, talk . . . that's all you boys do.
Why don't you both strap in and prove who's better?
We'll let the camera here be the judge.

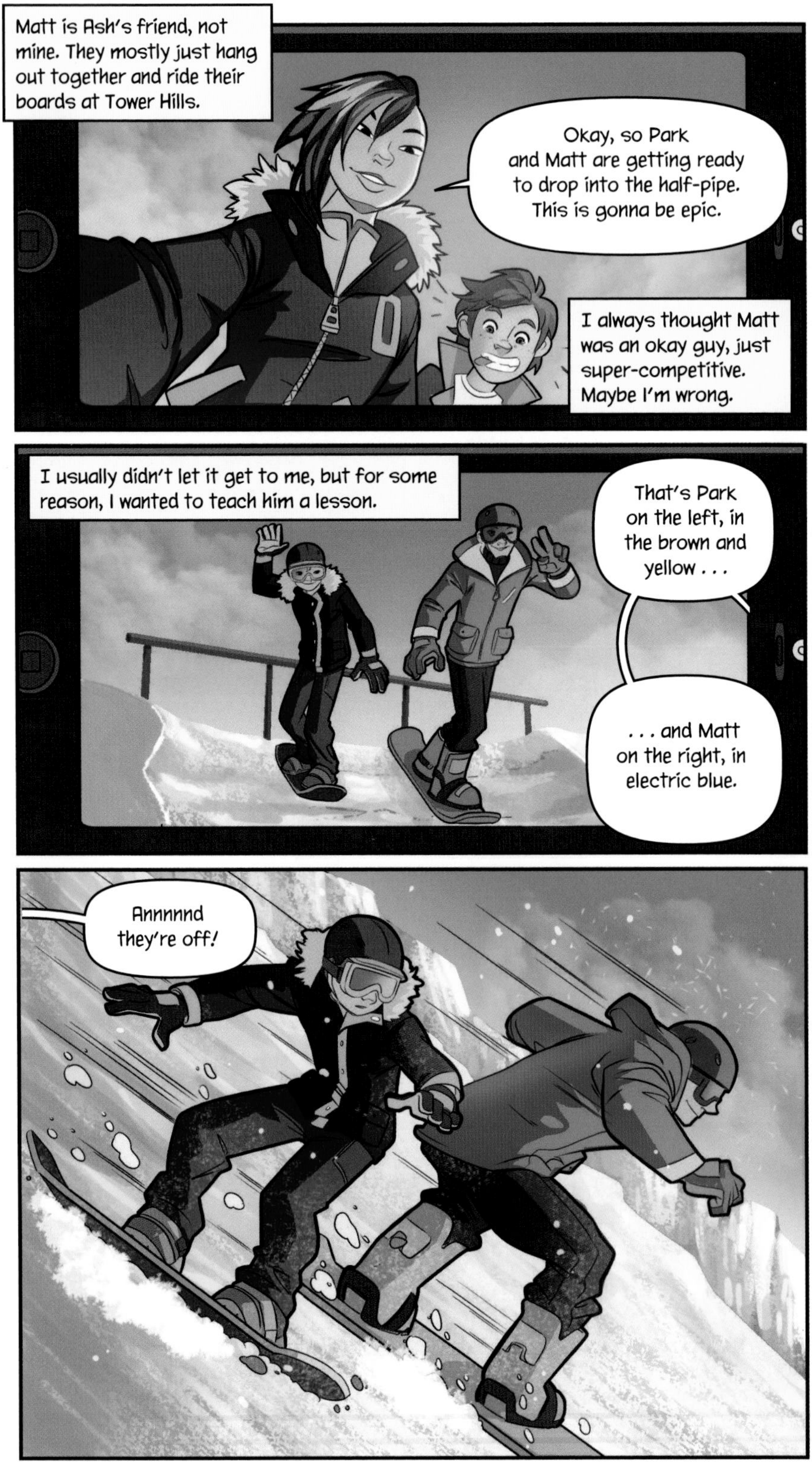
Matt is Ash's friend, not mine. They mostly just hang out together and ride their boards at Tower Hills.
Okay, so Park and Matt are getting ready to drop into the half-pipe. This is gonna be epic.
I always thought Matt was an okay guy, just super-competitive. Maybe I'm wrong.
I usually didn't let it get to me, but for some reason, I wanted to teach him a lesson.
That's Park on the left, in the brown and yellow . . .
. . . and Matt on the right, in electric blue.
Annnnnd they're off!

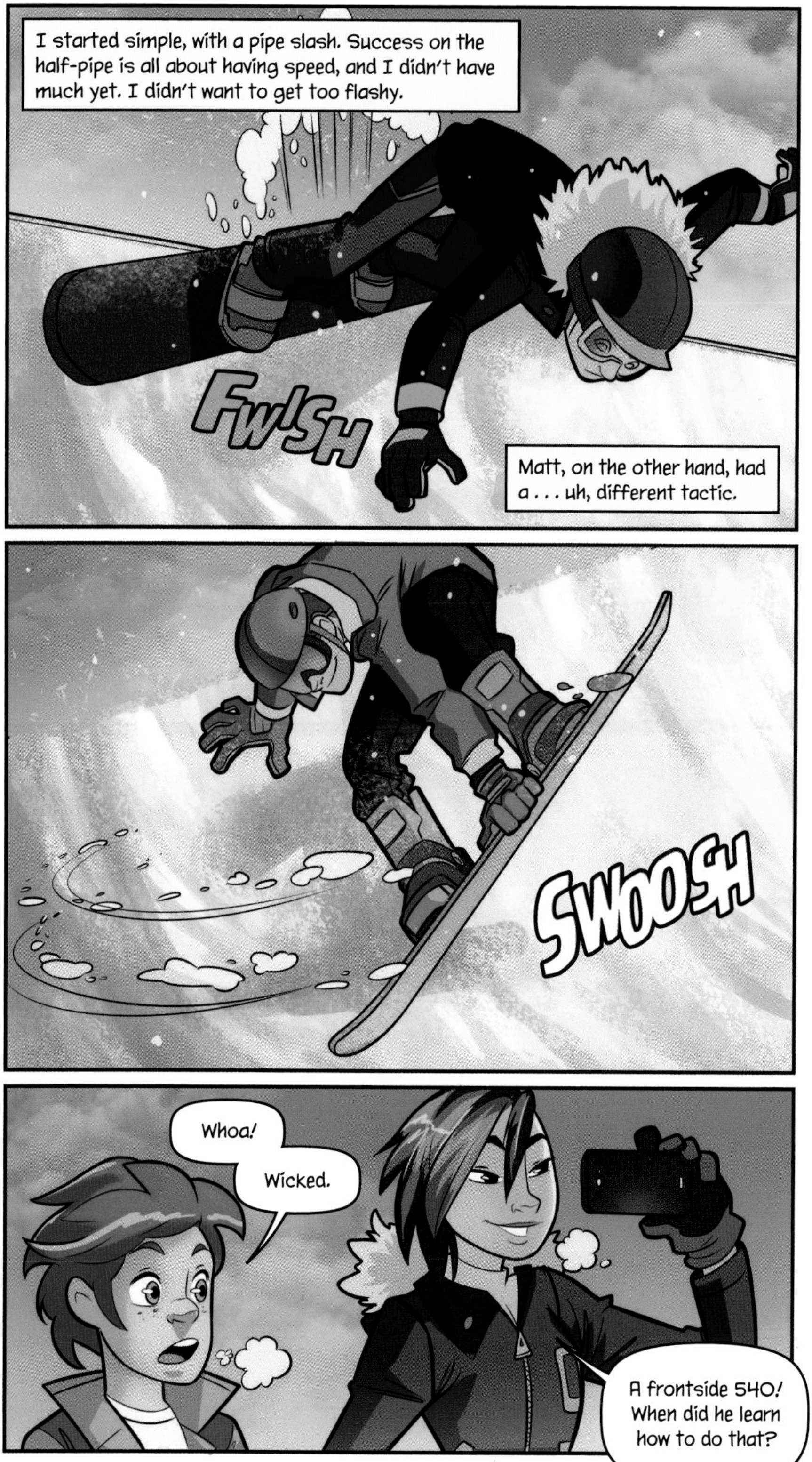
I started simple, with a pipe slash. Success on the half-pipe is all about having speed, and I didn't have much yet. I didn't want to get too flashy.
FWISH
Matt, on the other hand, had a . . . uh, different tactic.
SWOOSH
Whoa!
Wicked.
A frontside 540! When did he learn how to do that?

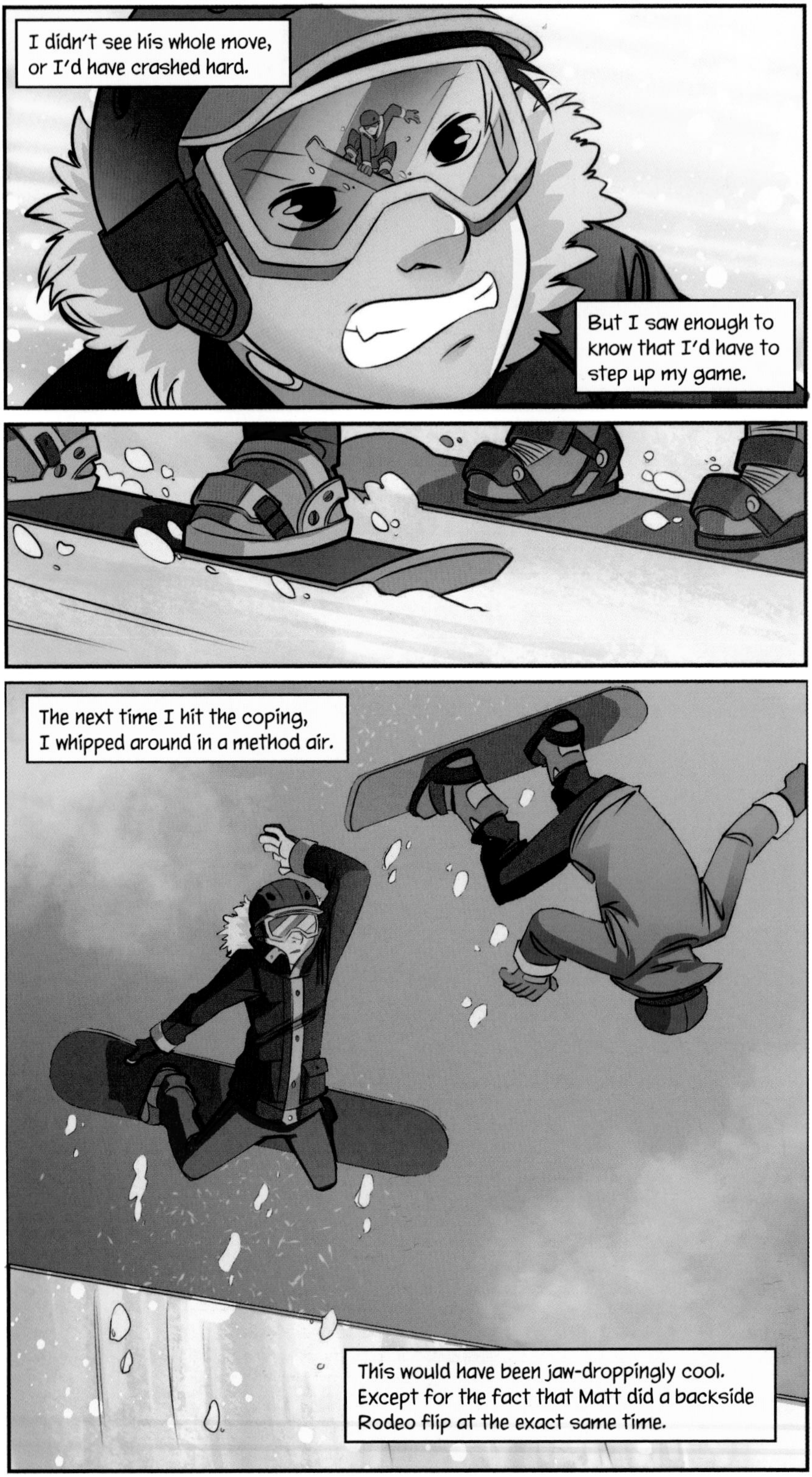
I didn't see his whole move, or I'd have crashed hard.
But I saw enough to know that I'd have to step up my game.
The next time I hit the coping, I whipped around in a method air.
This would have been jaw-droppingly cool. Except for the fact that Matt did a backside Rodeo flip at the exact same time.

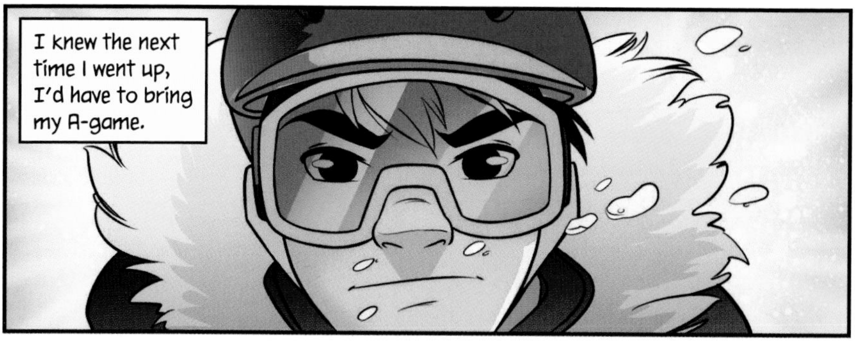
I knew the next time I went up, I'd have to bring my A-game.

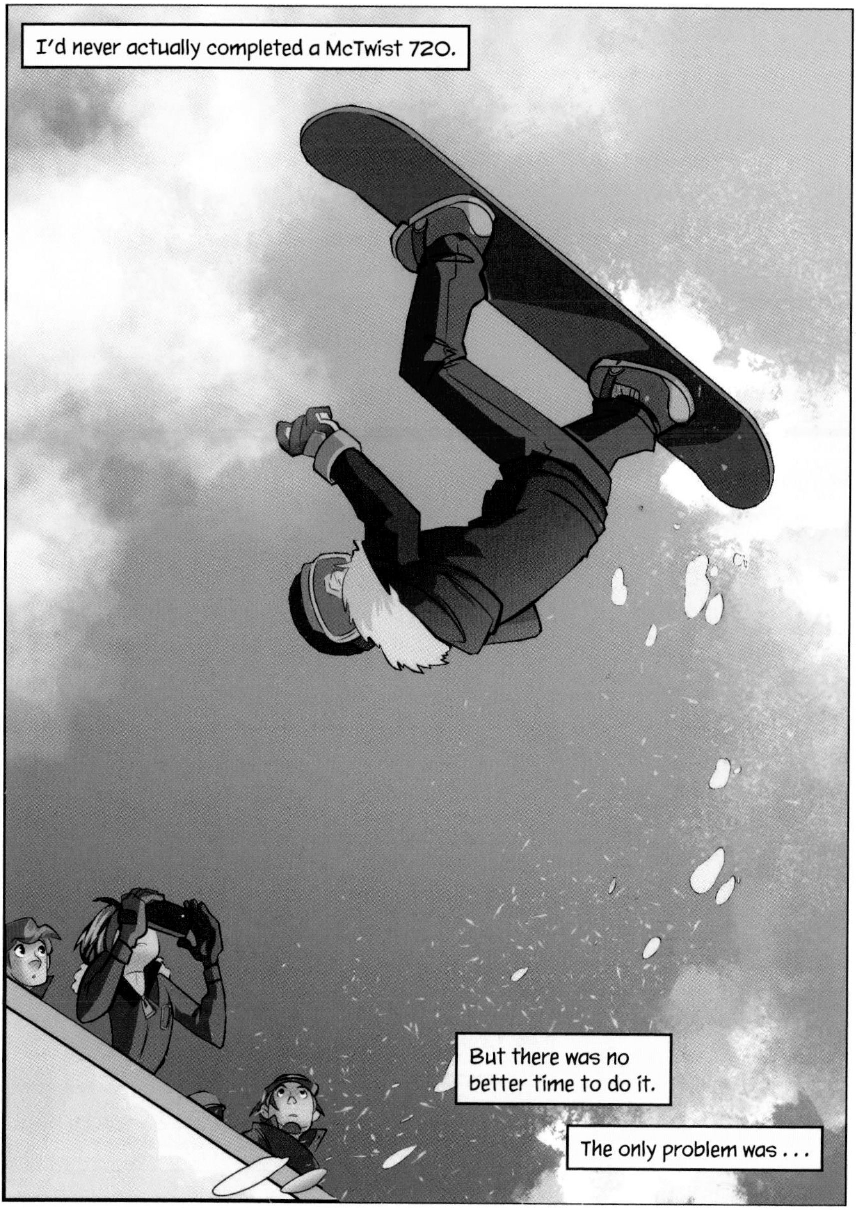
I'd never actually completed a McTwist 720.
But there was no better time to do it.
The only problem was . . .

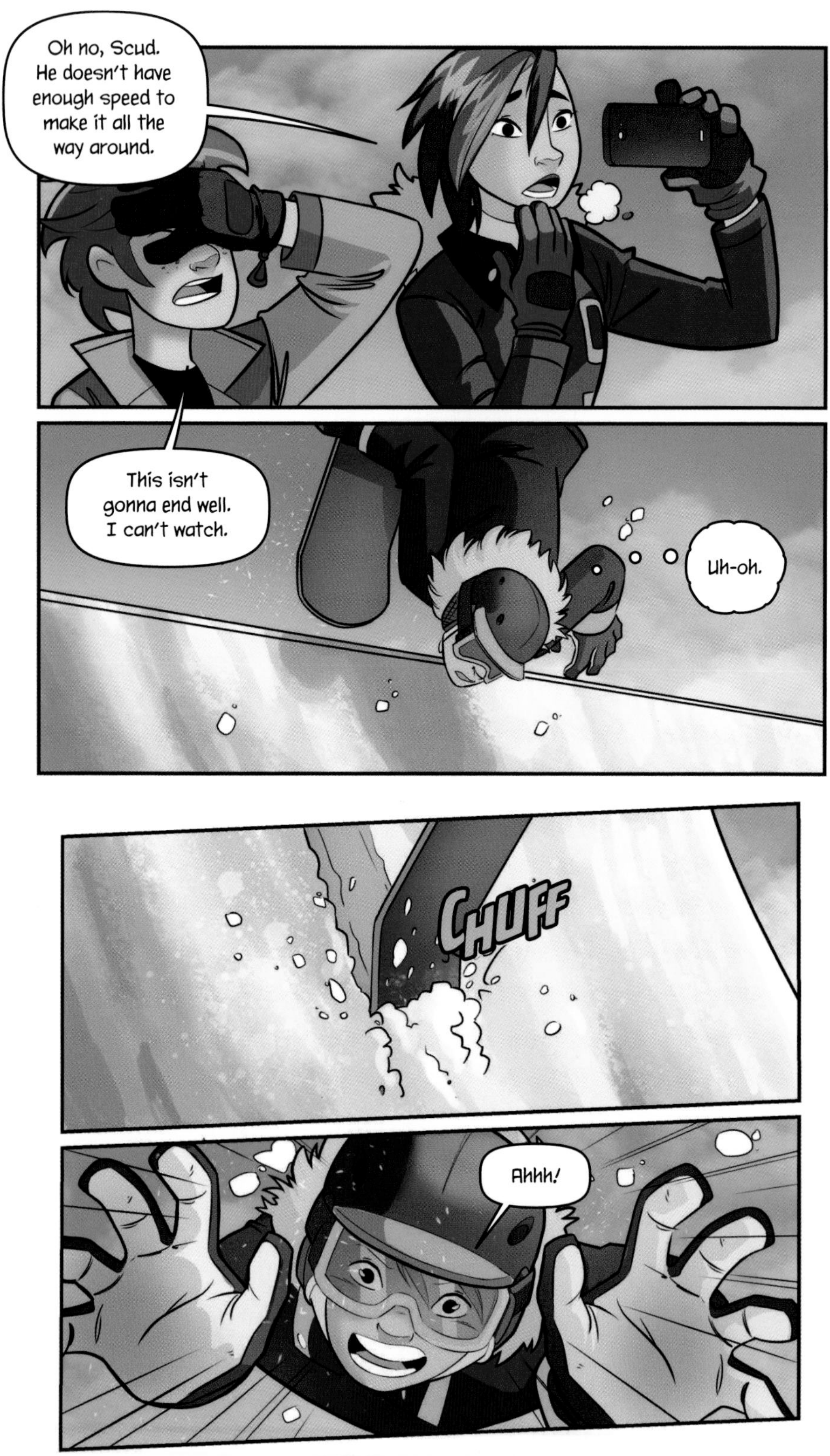
Oh no, Scud. He doesn't have enough speed to make it all the way around.
This isn't gonna end well. I can't watch.
Uh-oh.
CHUFF
Ahhh!

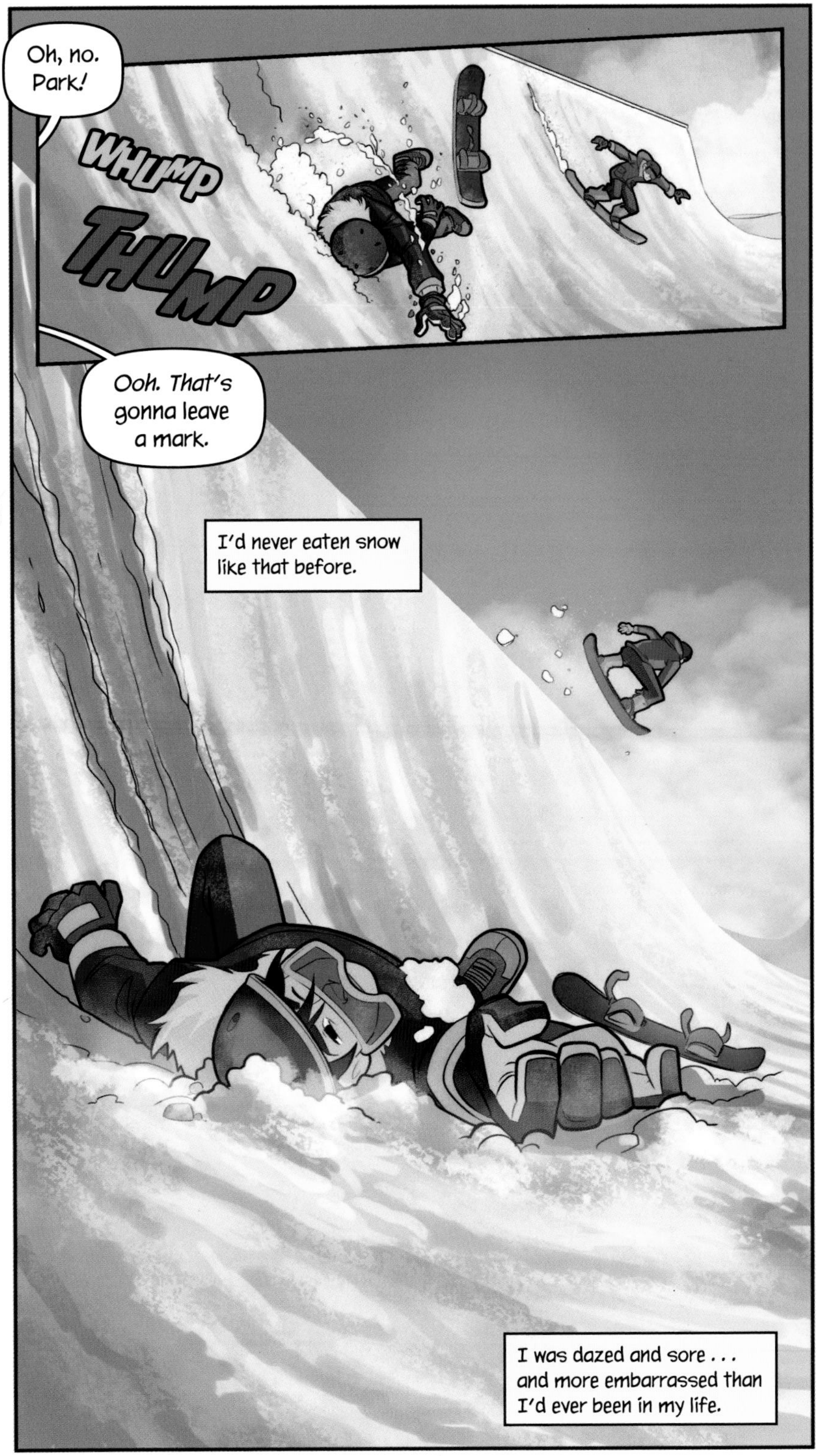
Oh, no. Park!
WHUMP
THUMP
Ooh. That's gonna leave a mark.
I'd never eaten snow like that before.
I was dazed and sore . . . and more embarrassed than I'd ever been in my life.

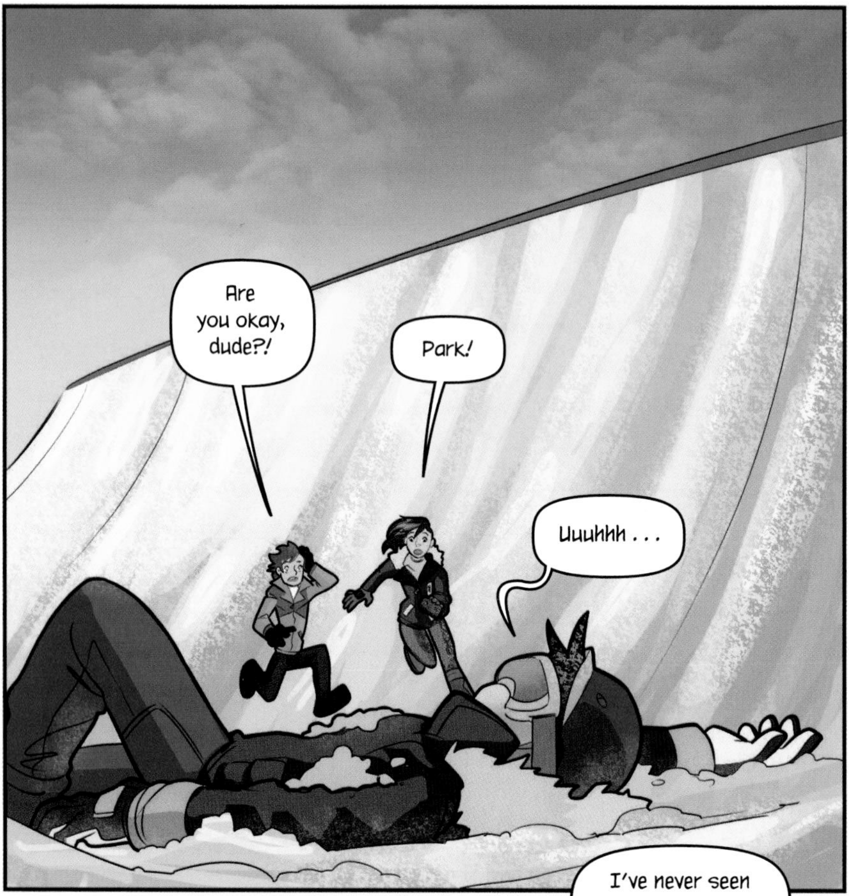
Are you okay, dude?!
Park!
Uuuhhh . . .

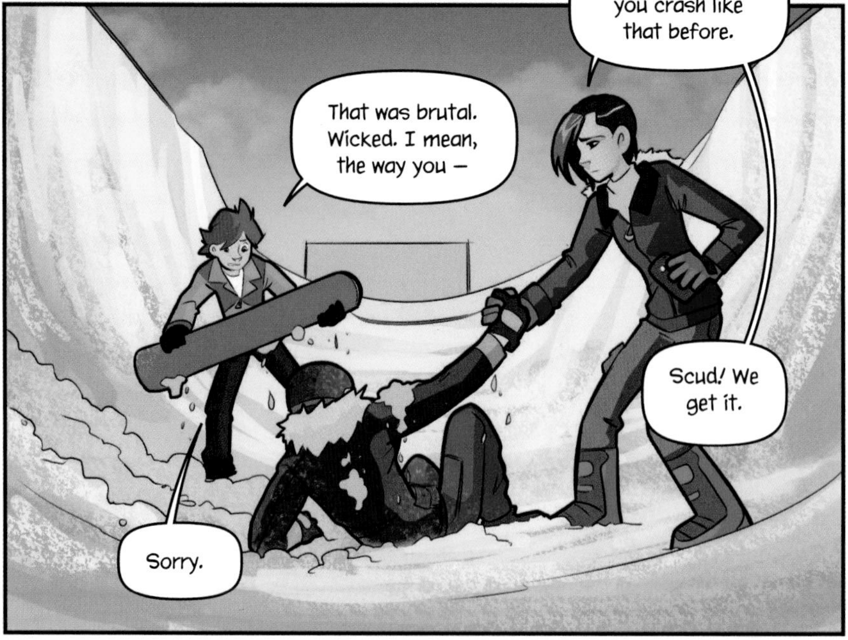
I've never seen you crash like that before.
That was brutal. Wicked. I mean, the way you —
Scud! We get it.
Sorry.

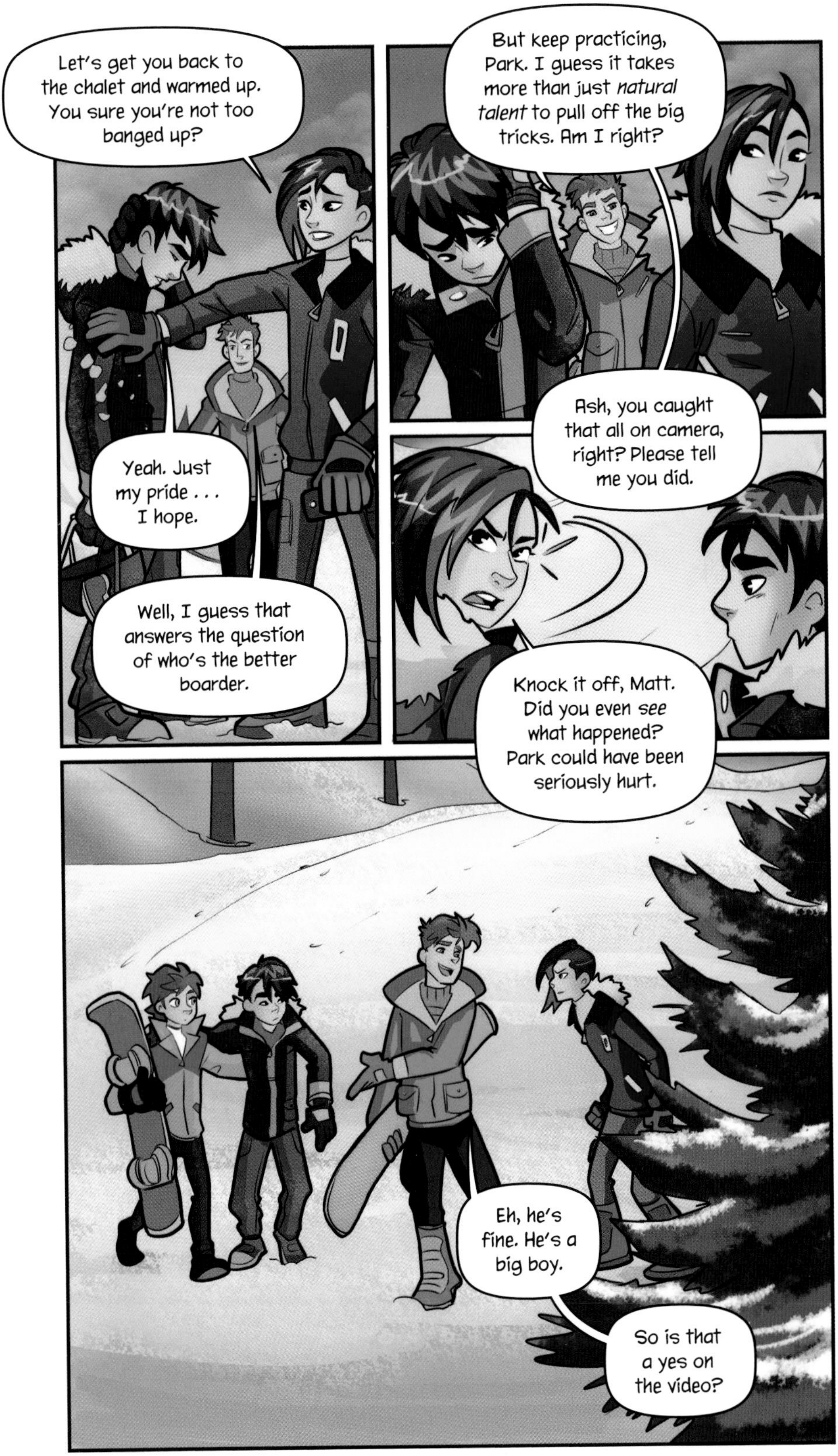
Let's get you back to the chalet and warmed up. You sure you're not too banged up?
Yeah. Just my pride . . . I hope.
Well, I guess that answers the question of who's the better boarder.
But keep practicing, Park. I guess it takes more than just *natural talent* to pull off the big tricks. Am I right?
Ash, you caught that all on camera, right? Please tell me you did.
Knock it off, Matt. Did you even *see* what happened? Park could have been seriously hurt.
Eh, he's fine. He's a big boy.
So is that a yes on the video?

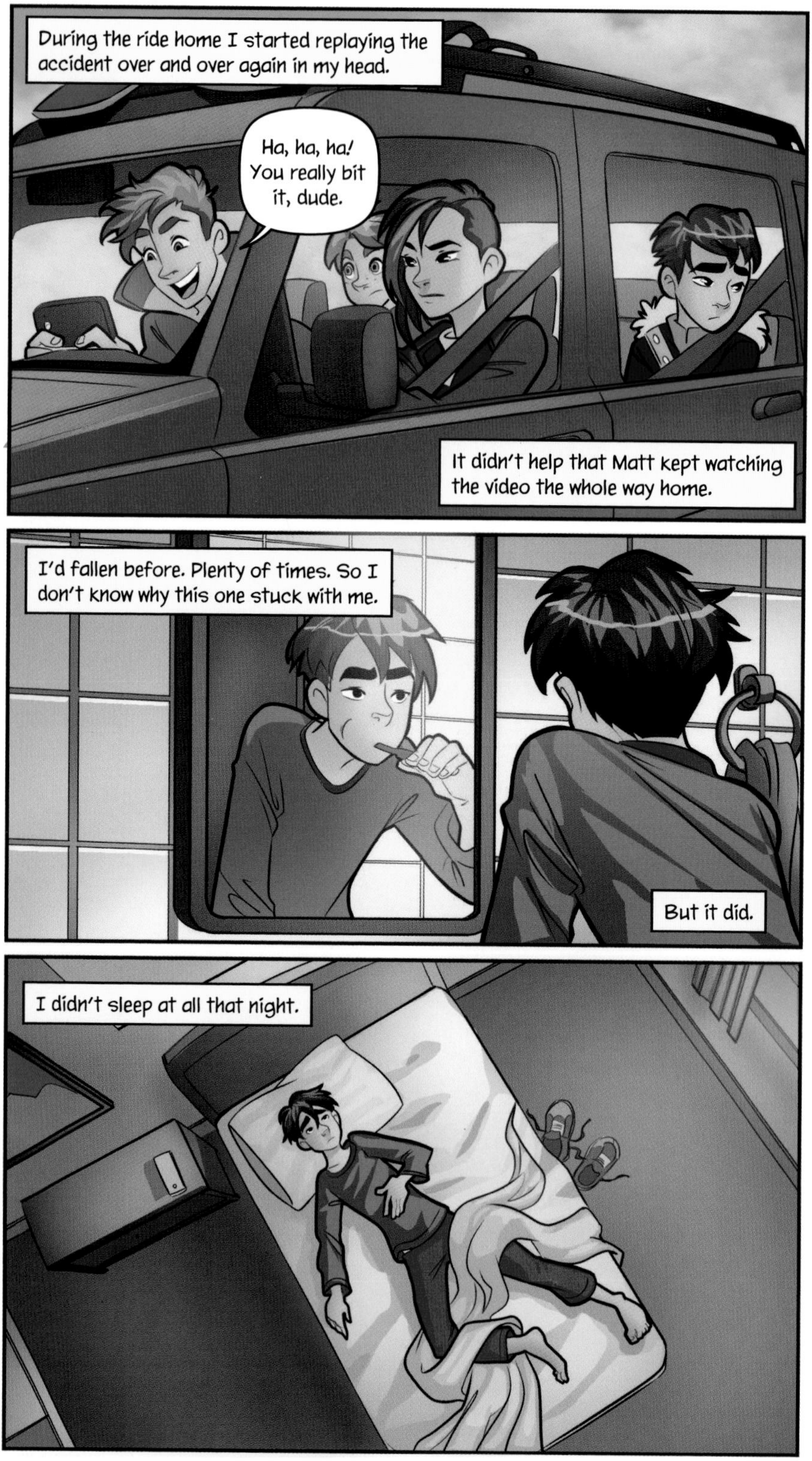
During the ride home I started replaying the accident over and over again in my head.
Ha, ha, ha! You really bit it, dude.
It didn't help that Matt kept watching the video the whole way home.
I'd fallen before. Plenty of times. So I don't know why this one stuck with me.
But it did.
I didn't sleep at all that night.

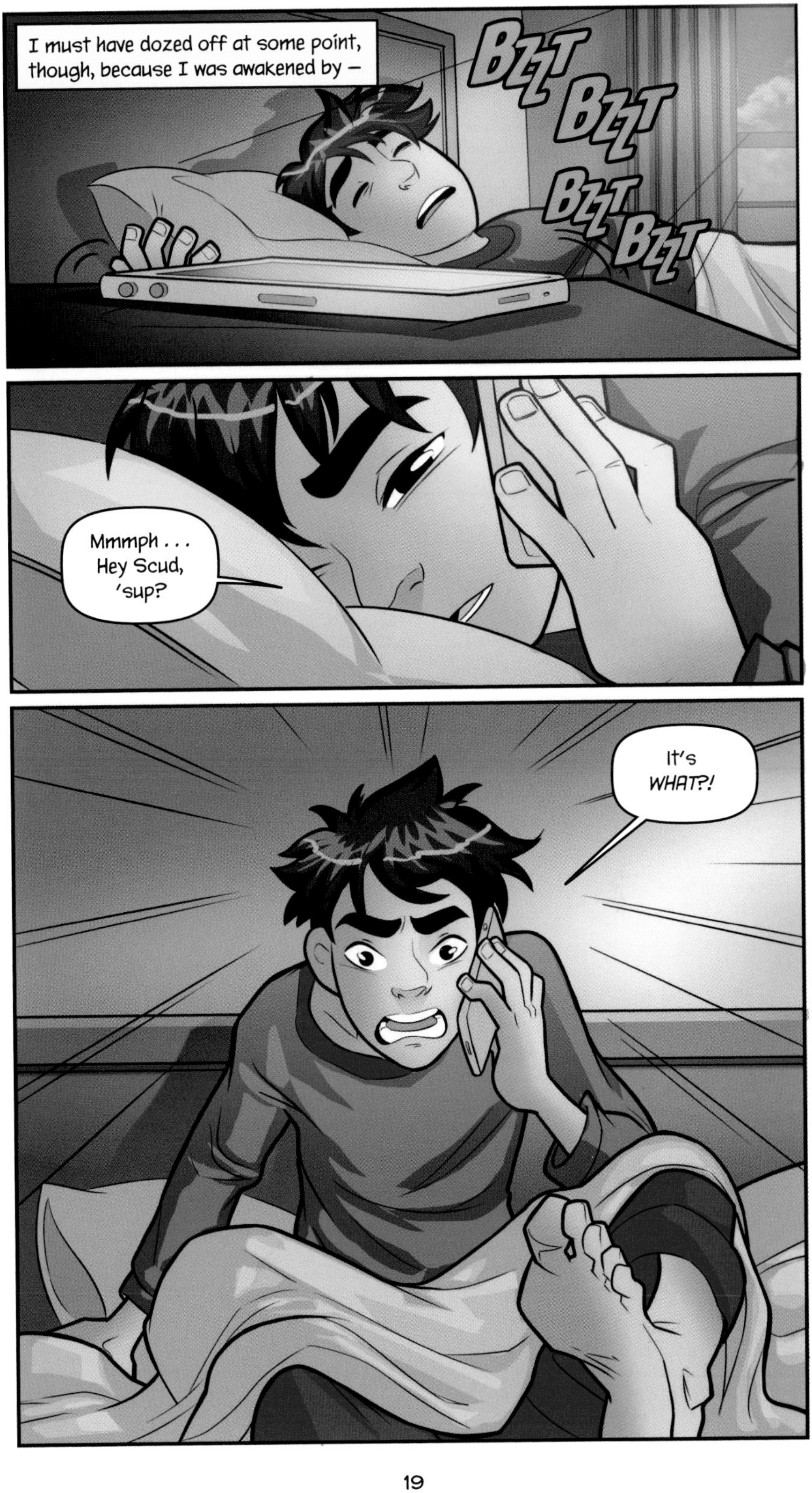

I must have dozed off at some point, though, because I was awakened by —
BZZT BZZT BZZT BZZT
Mmmph . . . Hey Scud, 'sup?
It's WHAT?!

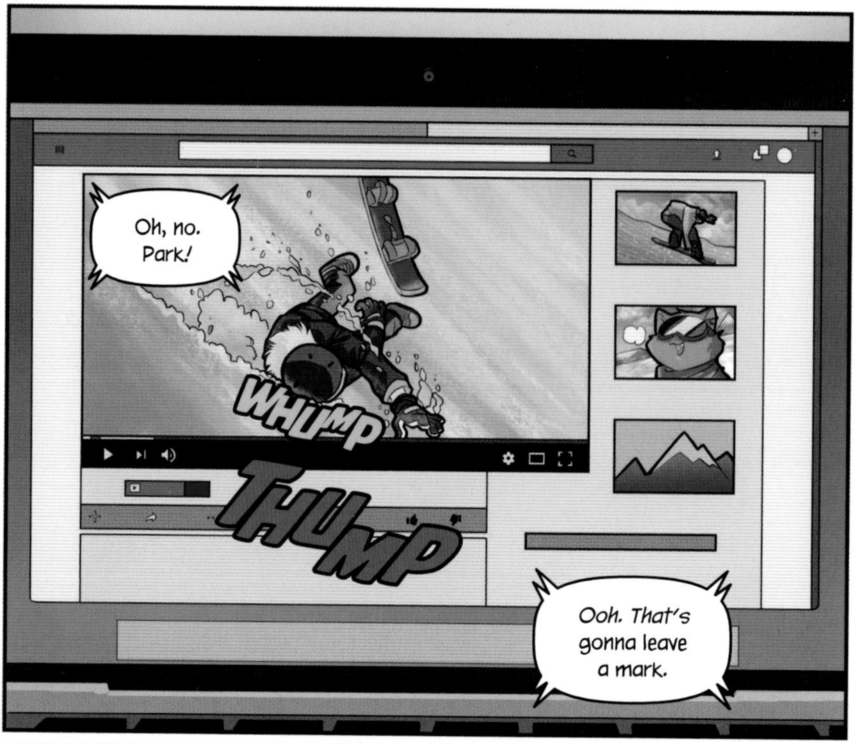
Oh, no. Park!
WHUMP
THUMP
Ooh. That's gonna leave a mark.

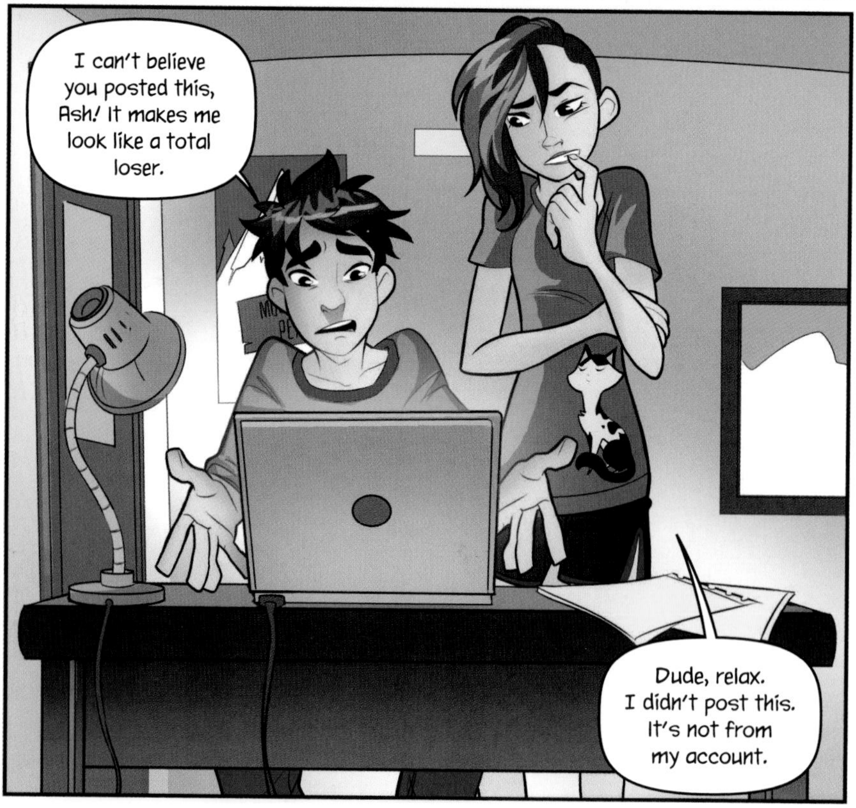
I can't believe you posted this, Ash! It makes me look like a total loser.
Dude, relax. I didn't post this. It's not from my account.

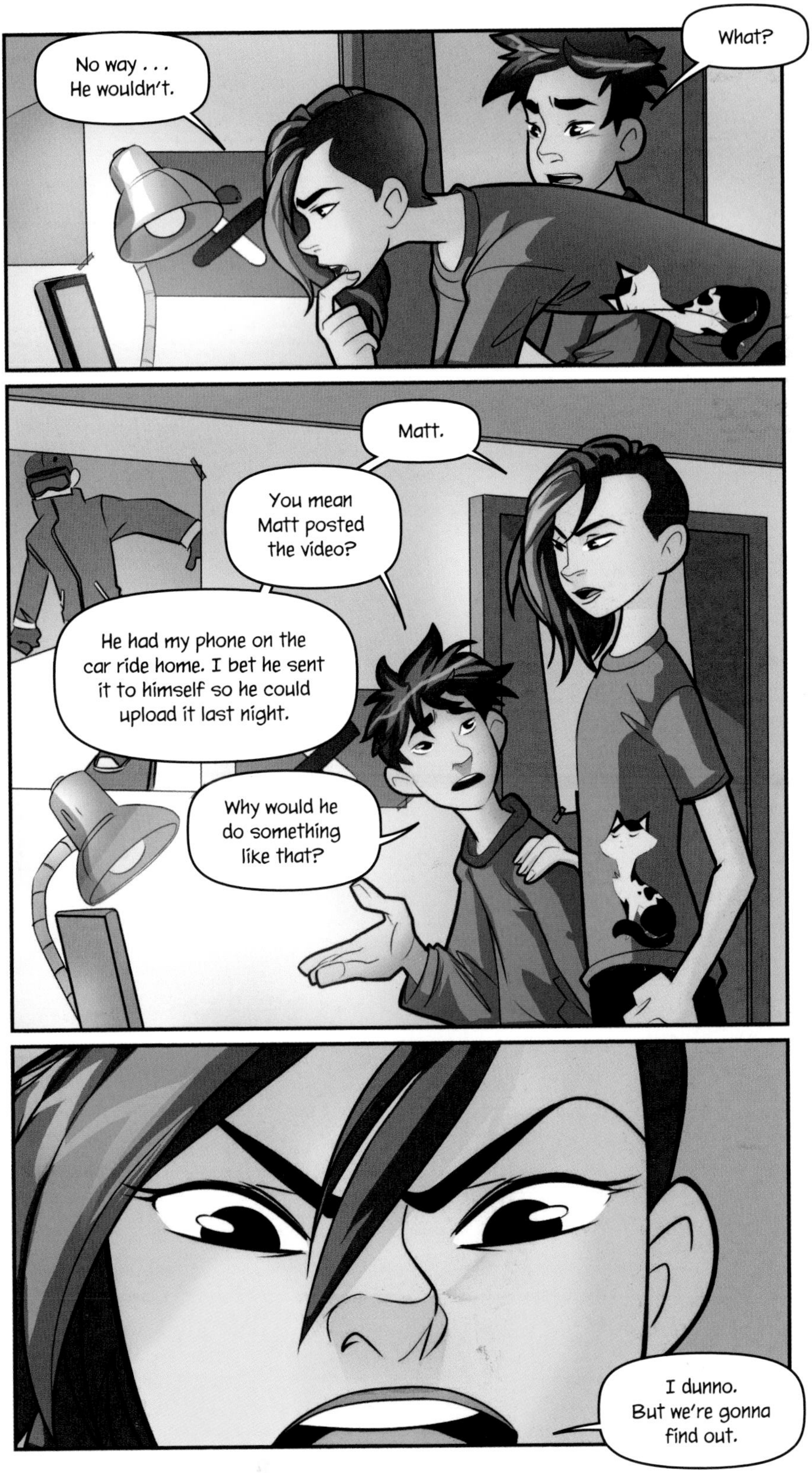
No way . . . He wouldn't.
What?
Matt.
You mean Matt posted the video?
He had my phone on the car ride home. I bet he sent it to himself so he could upload it last night.
Why would he do something like that?
I dunno. But we're gonna find out.

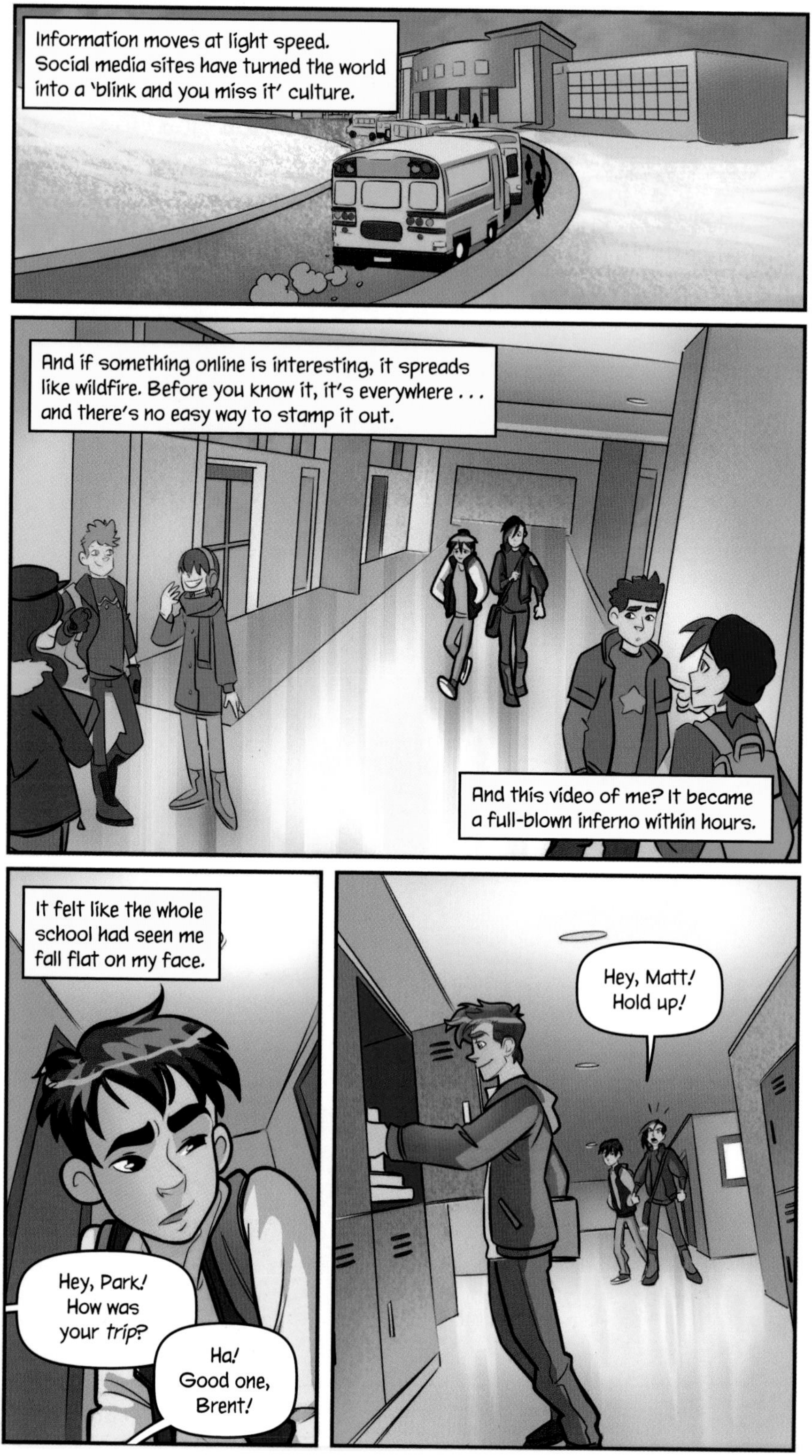
Information moves at light speed. Social media sites have turned the world into a 'blink and you miss it' culture.
And if something online is interesting, it spreads like wildfire. Before you know it, it's everywhere . . . and there's no easy way to stamp it out.
And this video of me? It became a full-blown inferno within hours.
It felt like the whole school had seen me fall flat on my face.
Hey, Park! How was your *trip*?
Ha! Good one, Brent!
Hey, Matt! Hold up!

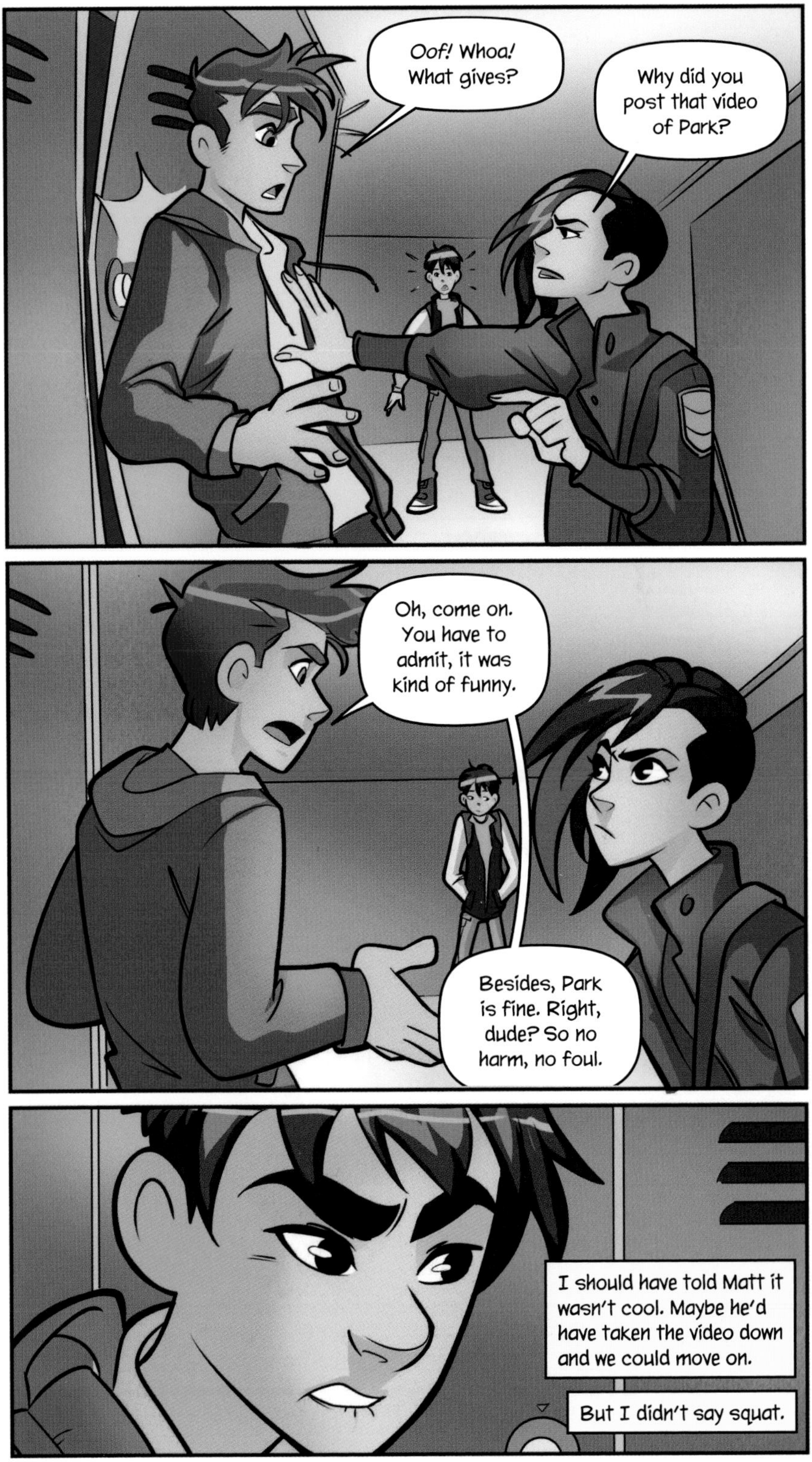
Oof! Whoa! What gives?
Why did you post that video of Park?
Oh, come on. You have to admit, it was kind of funny.
Besides, Park is fine. Right, dude? So no harm, no foul.
I should have told Matt it wasn't cool. Maybe he'd have taken the video down and we could move on.
But I didn't say squat.

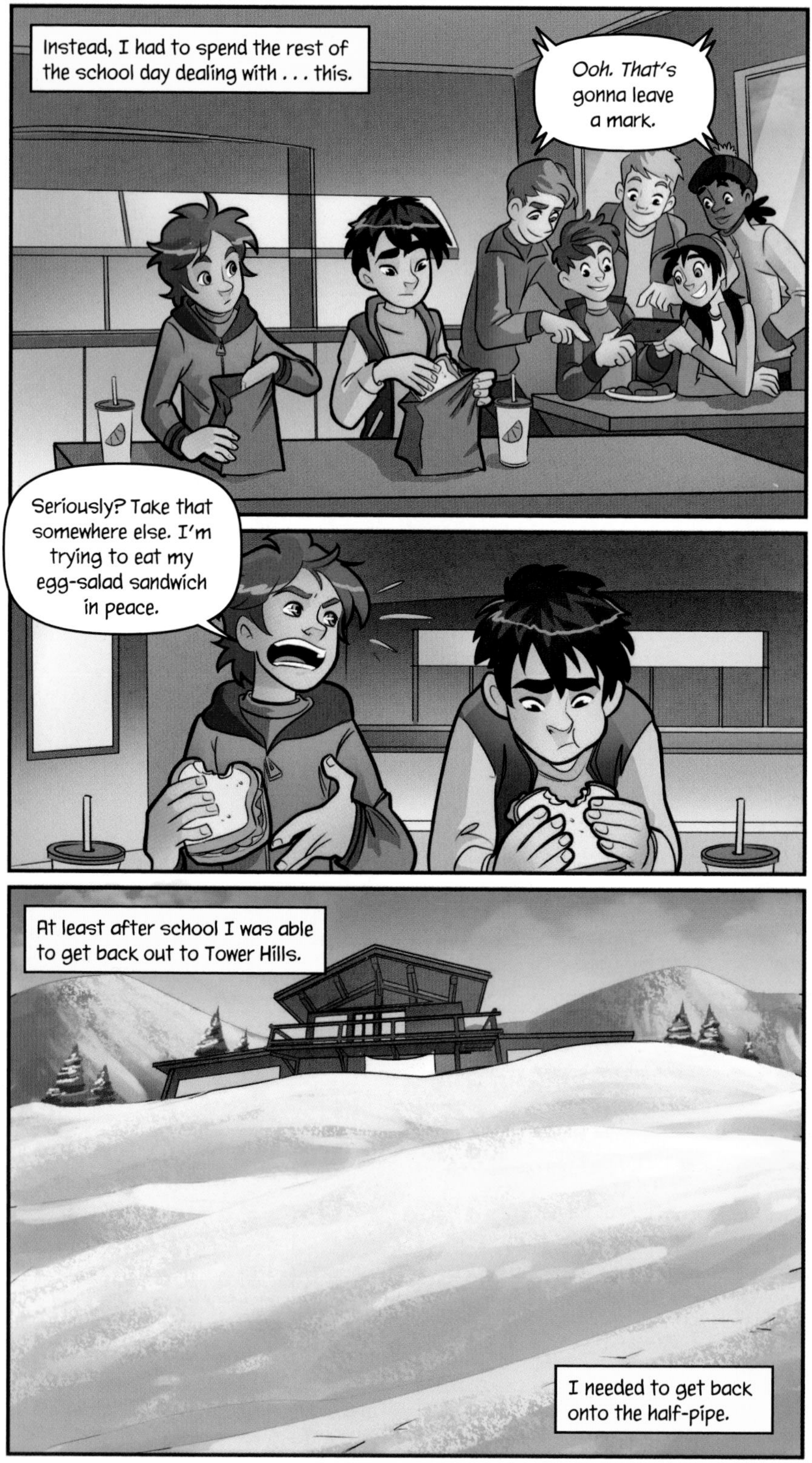
Instead, I had to spend the rest of the school day dealing with . . . this.
Ooh. That's gonna leave a mark.
Seriously? Take that somewhere else. I'm trying to eat my egg-salad sandwich in peace.
At least after school I was able to get back out to Tower Hills.
I needed to get back onto the half-pipe.

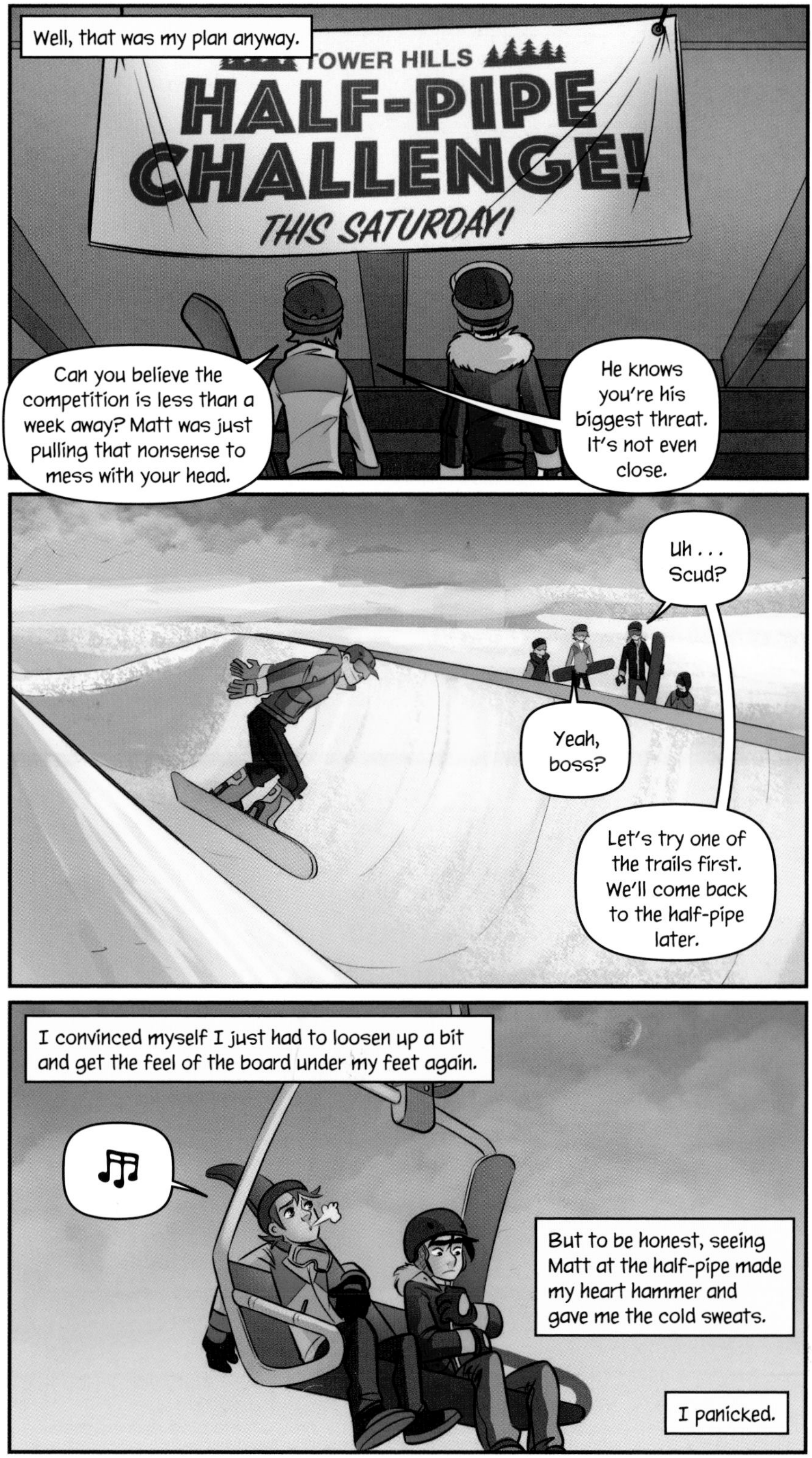
Well, that was my plan anyway.
TOWER HILLS
HALF-PIPE CHALLENGE!
THIS SATURDAY!
Can you believe the competition is less than a week away? Matt was just pulling that nonsense to mess with your head.
He knows you're his biggest threat. It's not even close.
Uh . . . Scud?
Yeah, boss?
Let's try one of the trails first. We'll come back to the half-pipe later.
I convinced myself I just had to loosen up a bit and get the feel of the board under my feet again.
♬
But to be honest, seeing Matt at the half-pipe made my heart hammer and gave me the cold sweats.
I panicked.

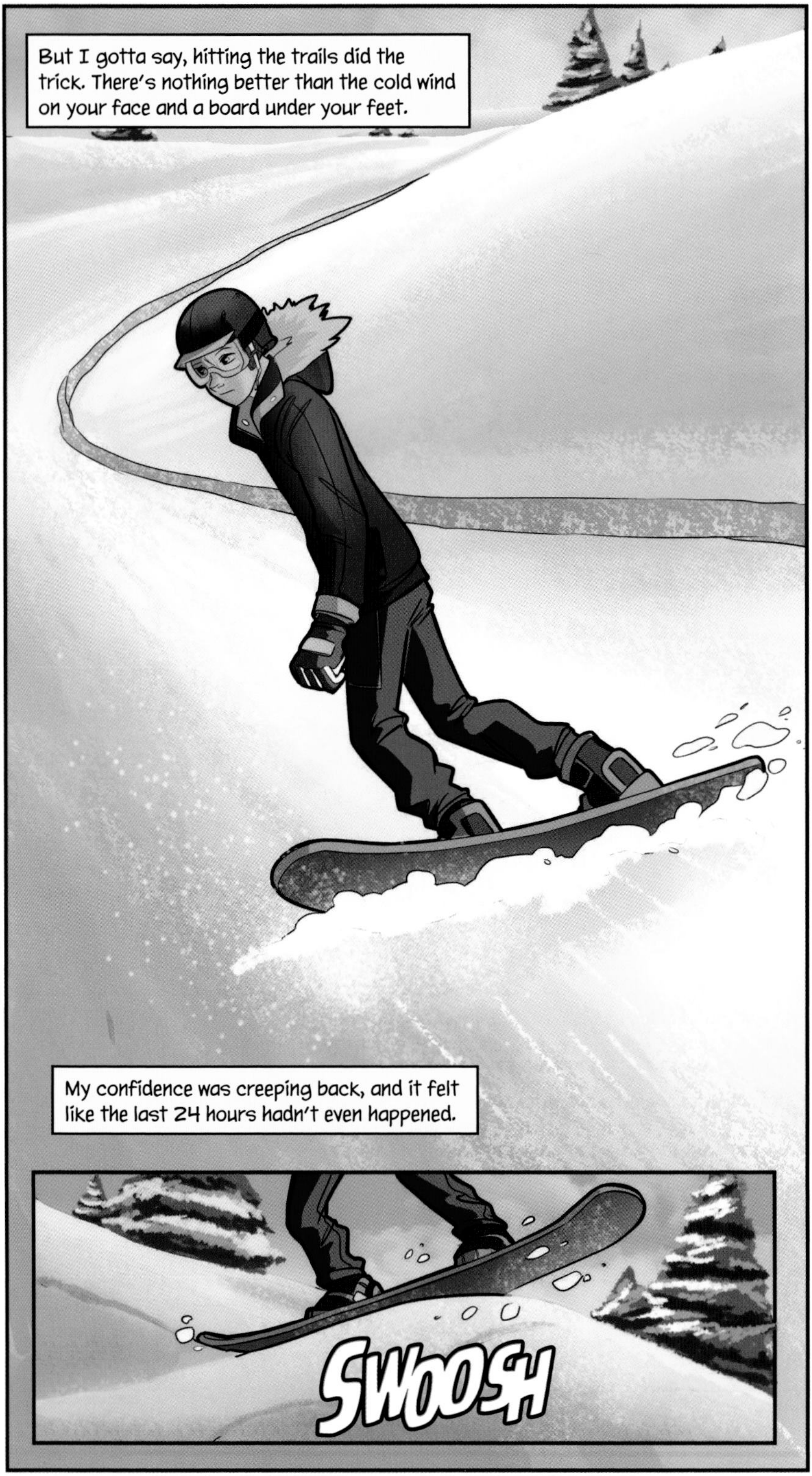
But I gotta say, hitting the trails did the trick. There's nothing better than the cold wind on your face and a board under your feet.
My confidence was creeping back, and it felt like the last 24 hours hadn't even happened.
SWOOSH

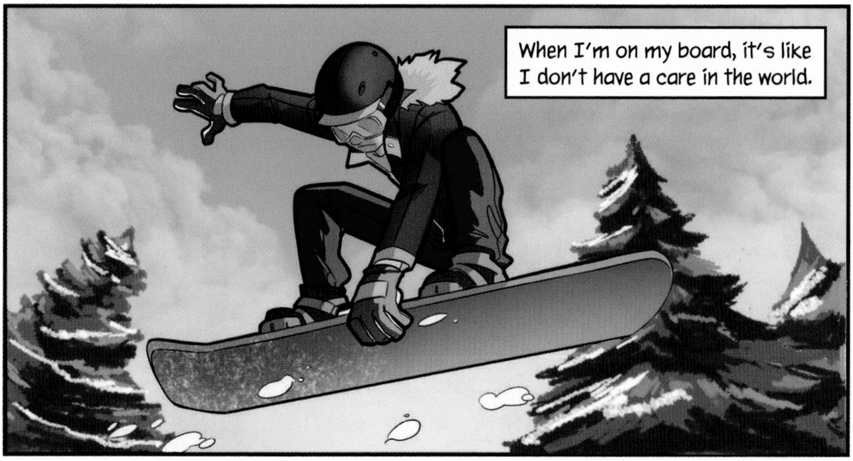
When I'm on my board, it's like I don't have a care in the world.

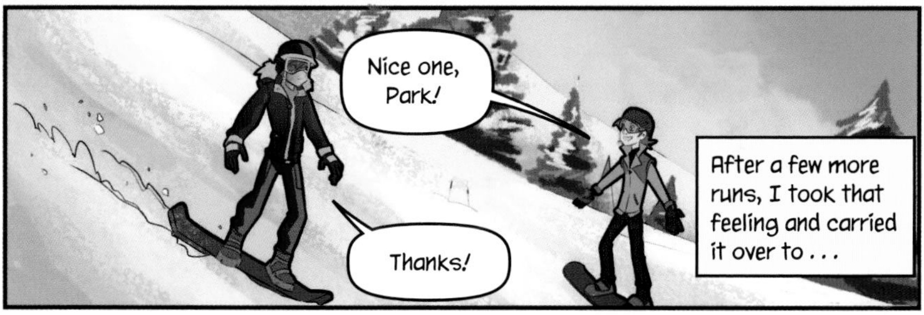
Nice one, Park!
Thanks!
After a few more runs, I took that feeling and carried it over to . . .

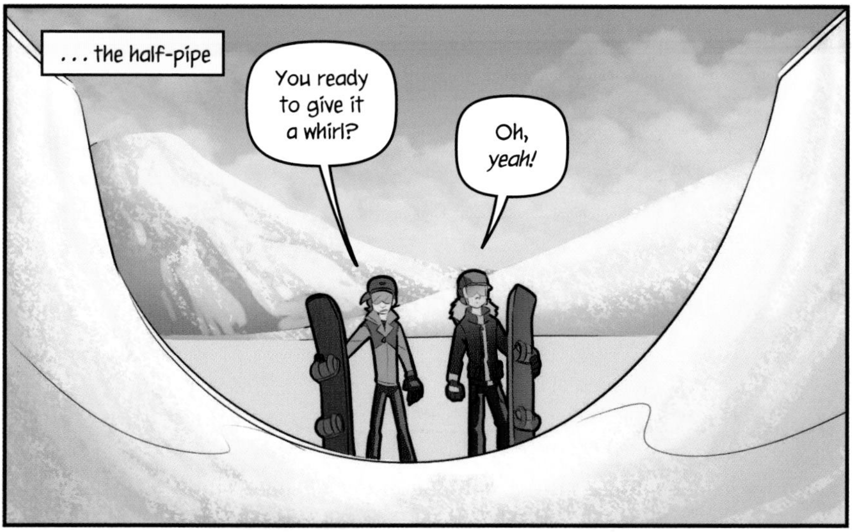
. . . the half-pipe
You ready to give it a whirl?
Oh, yeah!

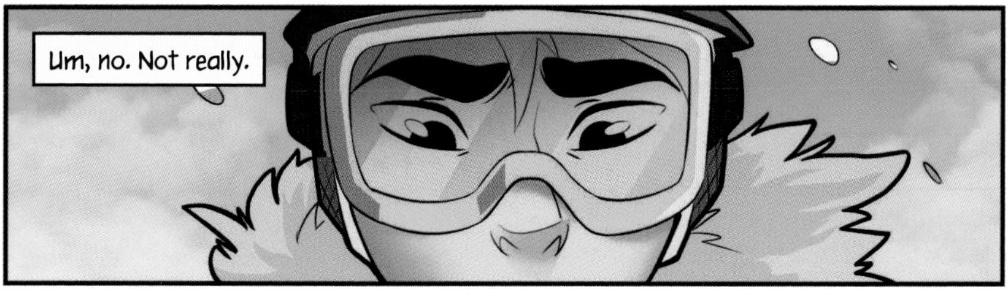
Um, no. Not really.

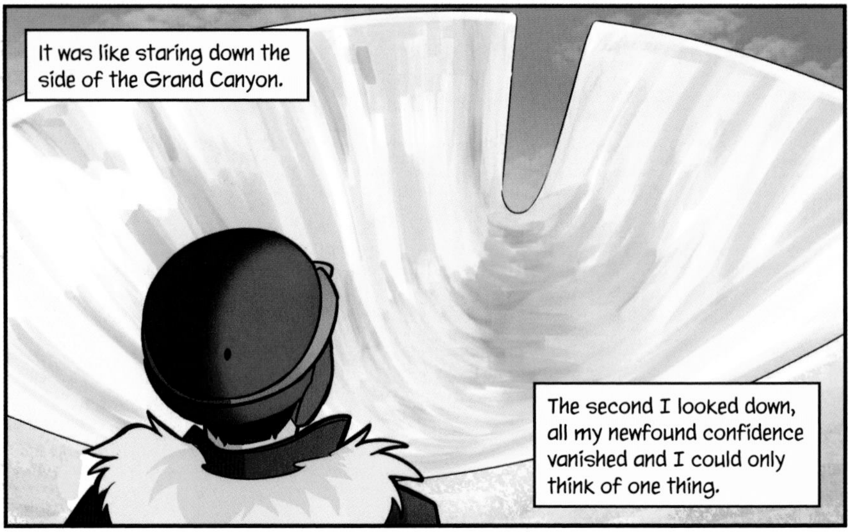
It was like staring down the side of the Grand Canyon.
The second I looked down, all my newfound confidence vanished and I could only think of one thing.

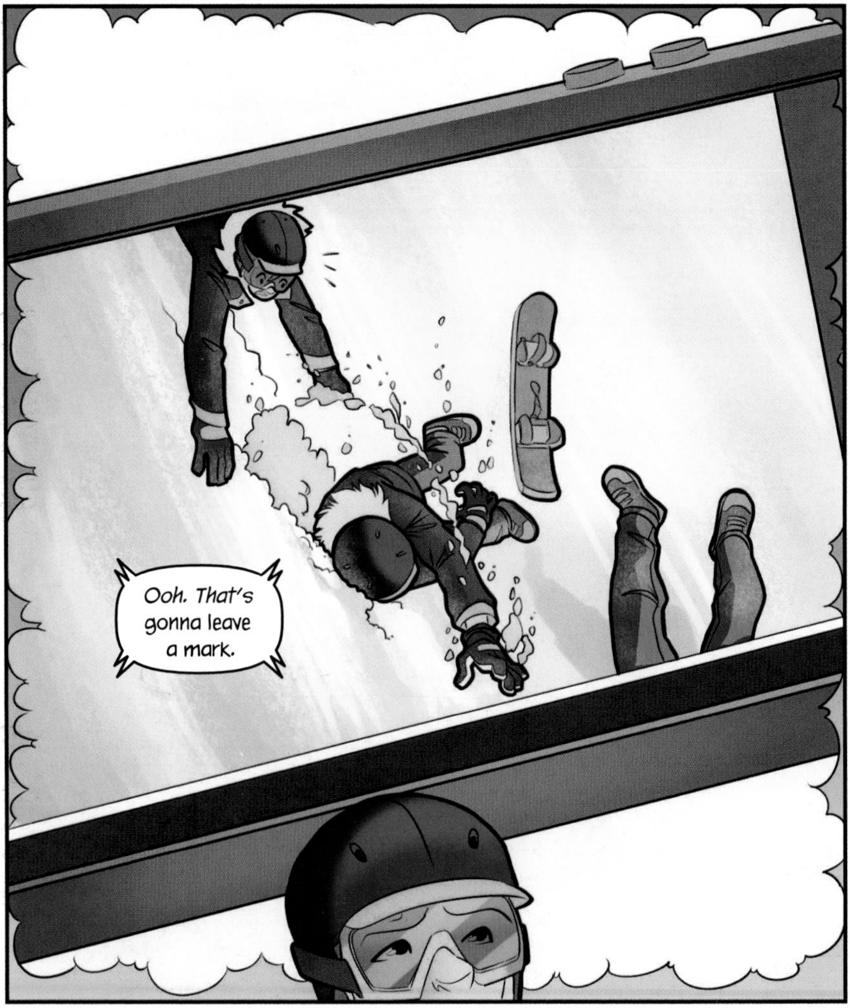
Ooh. That's gonna leave a mark.

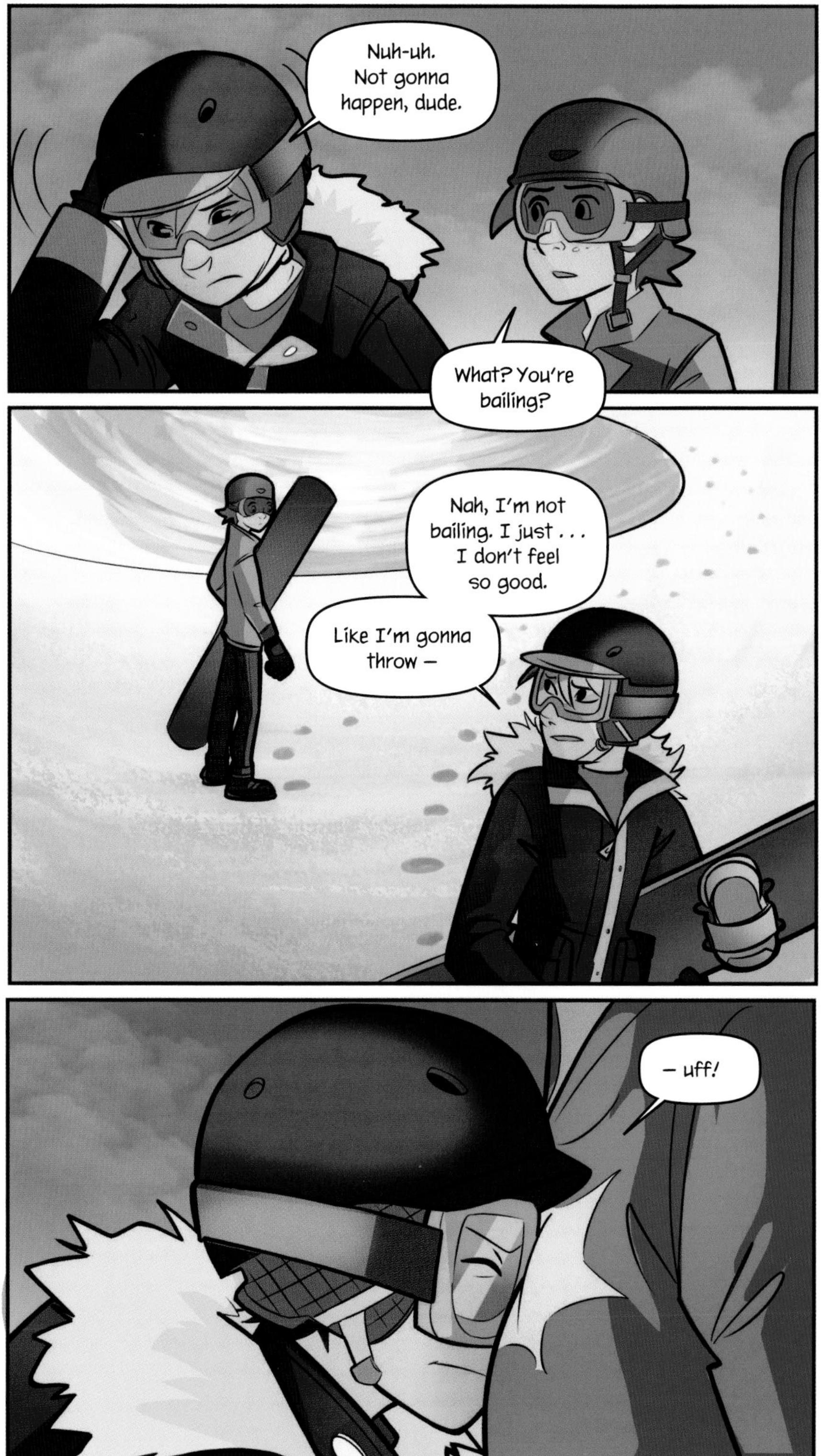
Nuh-uh. Not gonna happen, dude.
What? You're bailing?
Nah, I'm not bailing. I just . . . I don't feel so good.
Like I'm gonna throw –
– uff!

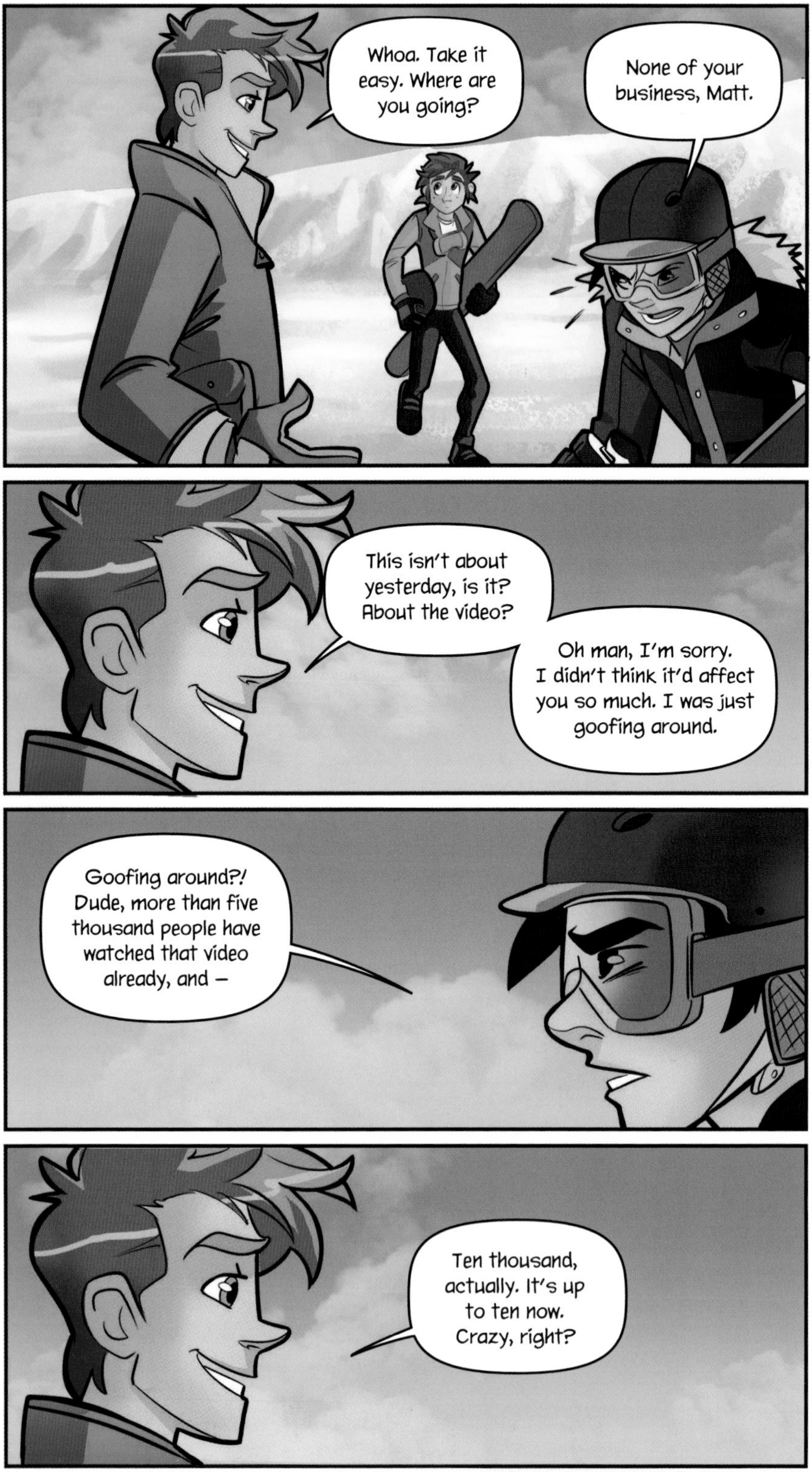
Whoa. Take it easy. Where are you going?
None of your business, Matt.
This isn't about yesterday, is it? About the video?
Oh man, I'm sorry. I didn't think it'd affect you so much. I was just goofing around.
Goofing around?! Dude, more than five thousand people have watched that video already, and –
Ten thousand, actually. It's up to ten now. Crazy, right?

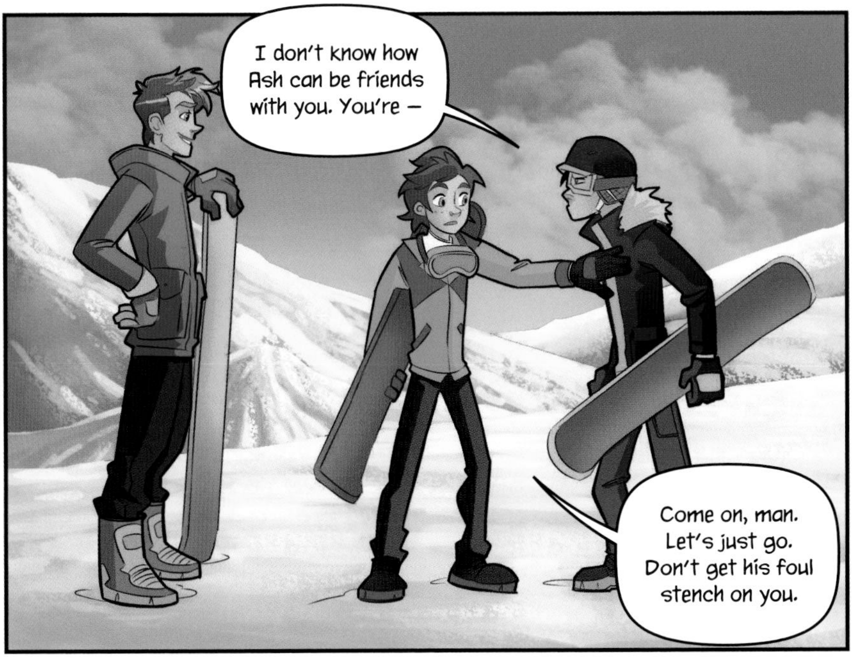
I don't know how Ash can be friends with you. You're —
Come on, man. Let's just go. Don't get his foul stench on you.

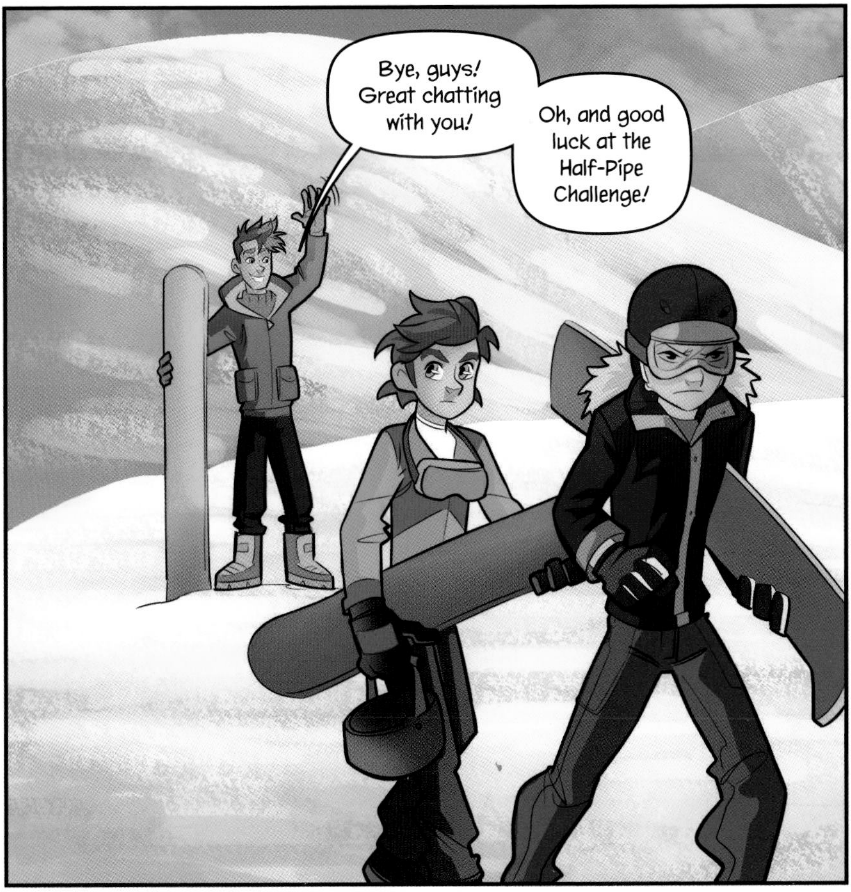
Bye, guys! Great chatting with you!
Oh, and good luck at the Half-Pipe Challenge!

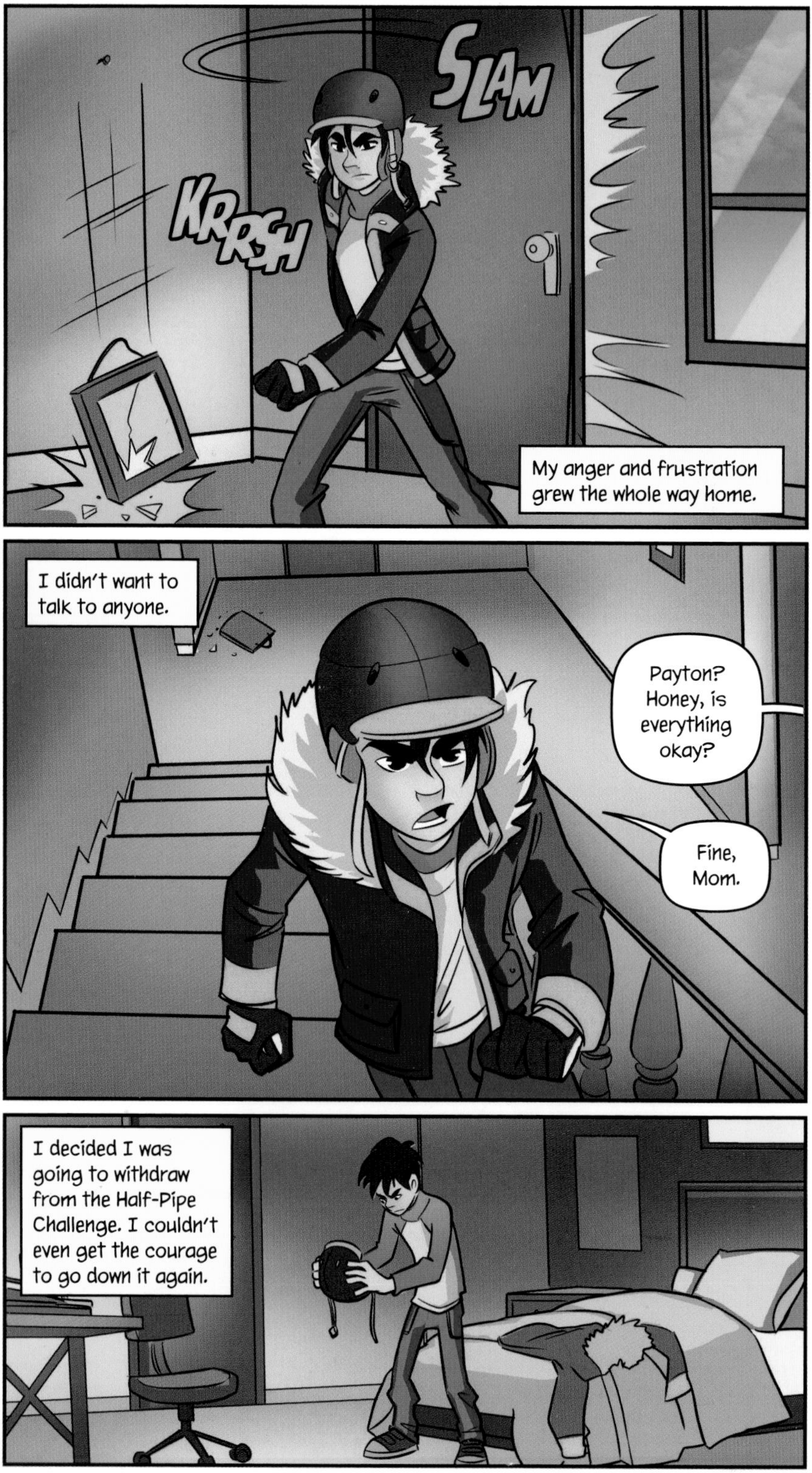
SLAM
KRRSH
My anger and frustration grew the whole way home.
I didn't want to talk to anyone.
Payton? Honey, is everything okay?
Fine, Mom.
I decided I was going to withdraw from the Half-Pipe Challenge. I couldn't even get the courage to go down it again.

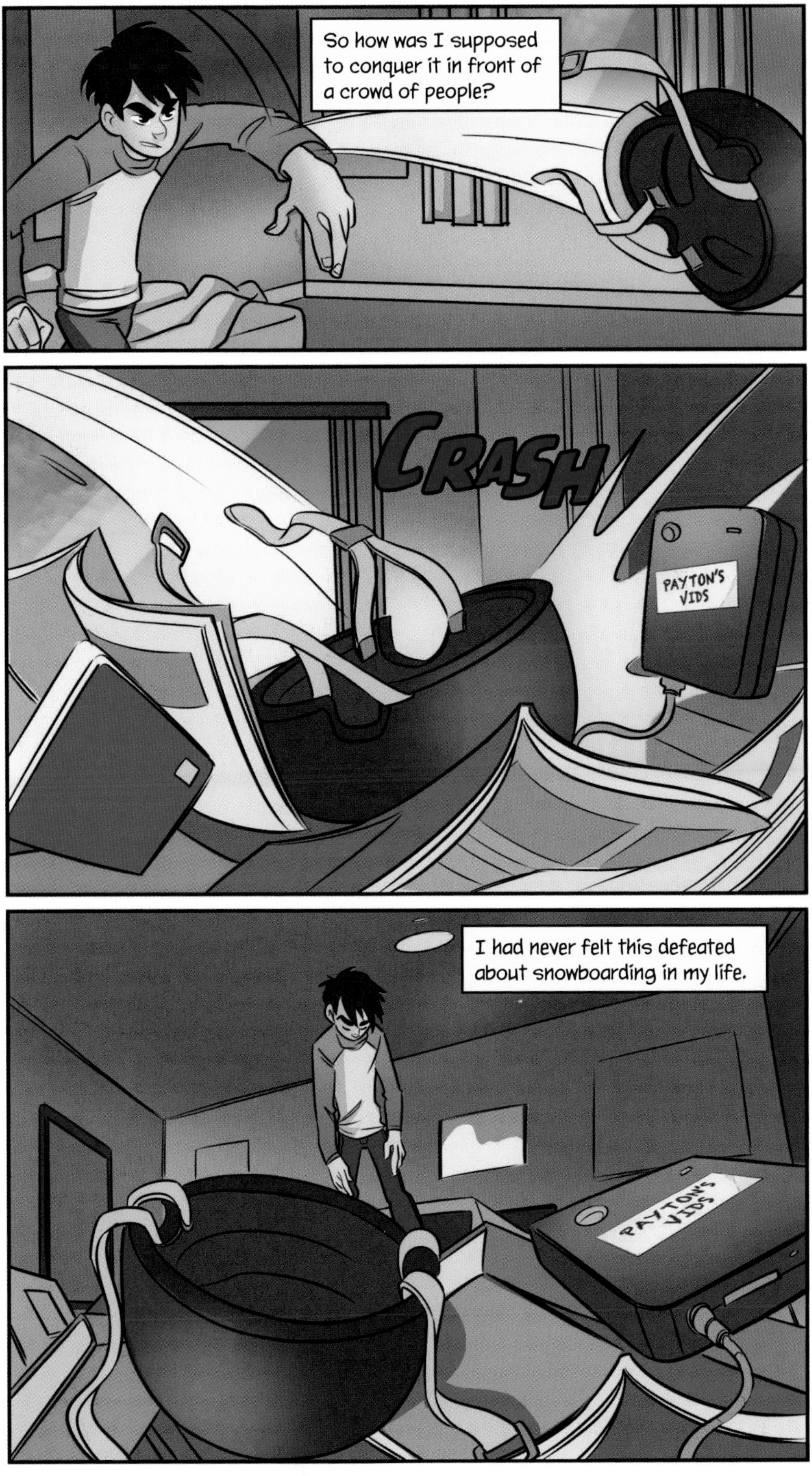
So how was I supposed to conquer it in front of a crowd of people?
CRASH
PAYTON'S VIDS
I had never felt this defeated about snowboarding in my life.
PAYTON'S VIDS

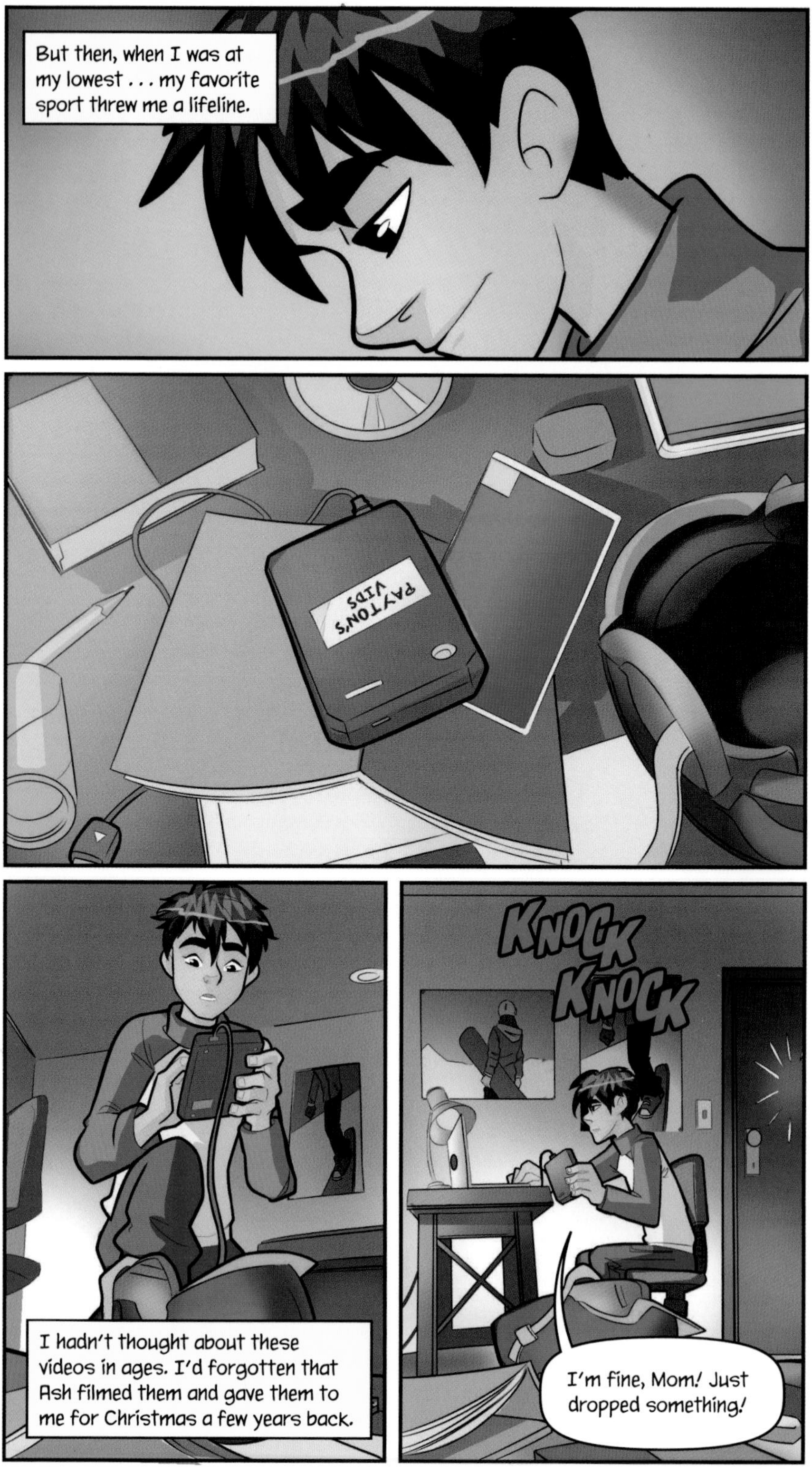
But then, when I was at my lowest . . . my favorite sport threw me a lifeline.
PAYTON'S VIDS
I hadn't thought about these videos in ages. I'd forgotten that Ash filmed them and gave them to me for Christmas a few years back.
KNOCK KNOCK
I'm fine, Mom! Just dropped something!

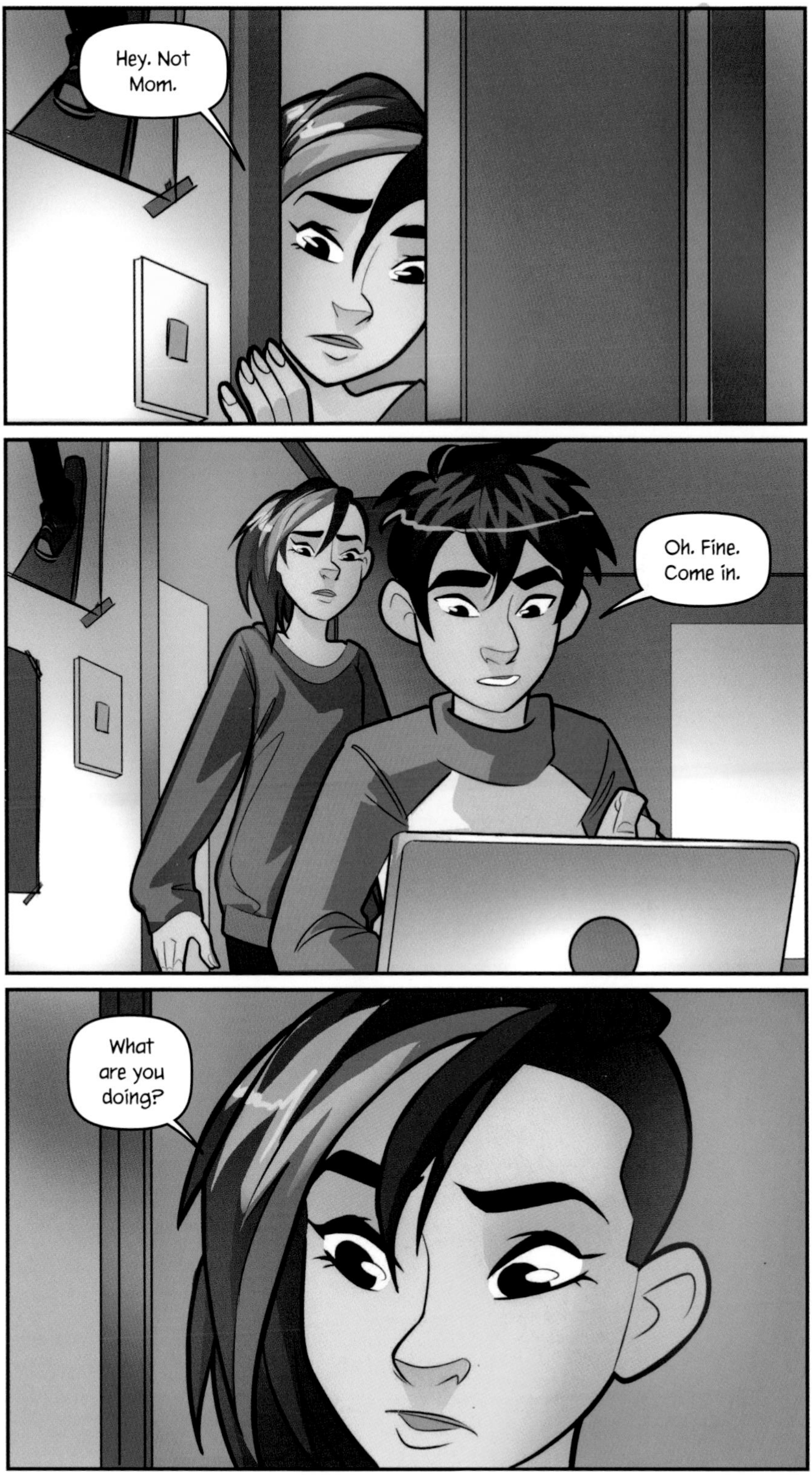
Hey. Not Mom.
Oh. Fine. Come in.
What are you doing?

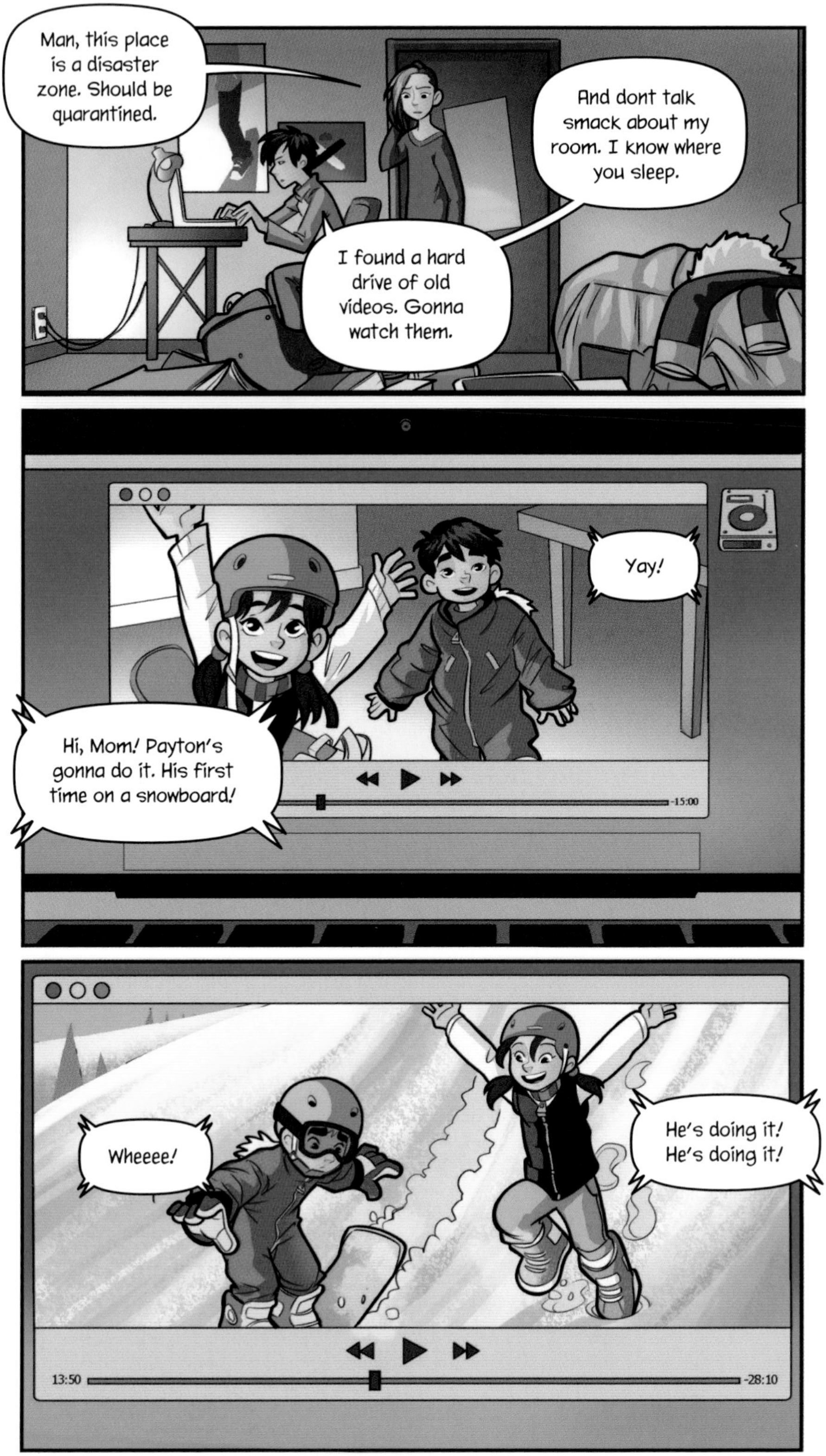
Man, this place is a disaster zone. Should be quarantined.
I found a hard drive of old videos. Gonna watch them.
And dont talk smack about my room. I know where you sleep.
Hi, Mom! Payton's gonna do it. His first time on a snowboard!
Yay!
-15:00
Wheeee!
He's doing it! He's doing it!
13:50
-28:10

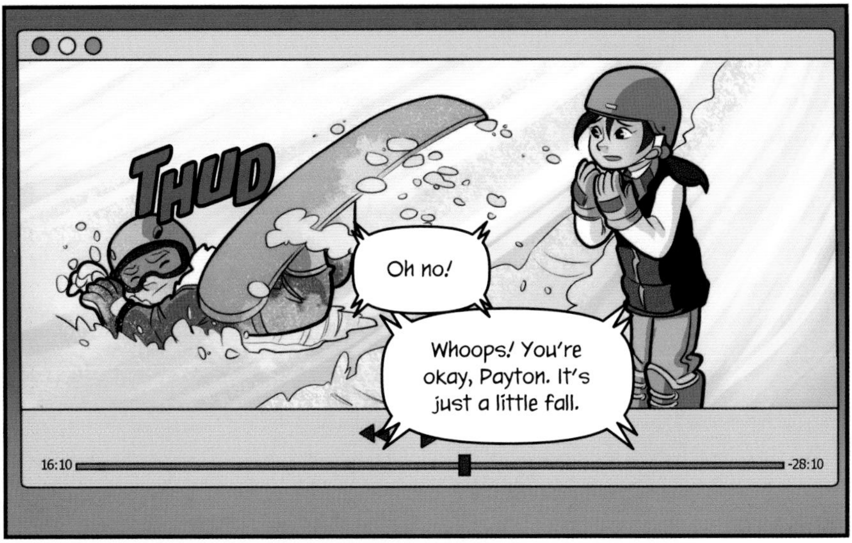
THUD
Oh no!
Whoops! You're okay, Payton. It's just a little fall.
16:10
-28:10

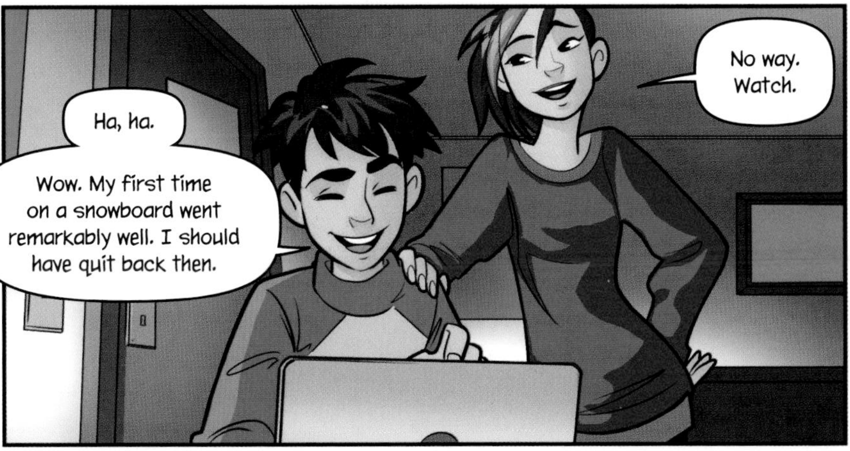
No way. Watch.
Ha, ha.
Wow. My first time on a snowboard went remarkably well. I should have quit back then.

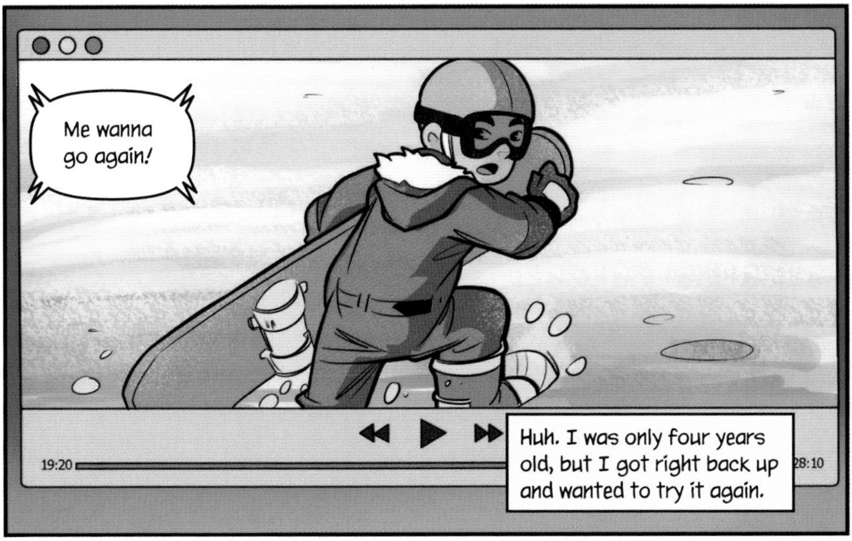
Me wanna go again!
19:20
Huh. I was only four years old, but I got right back up and wanted to try it again.

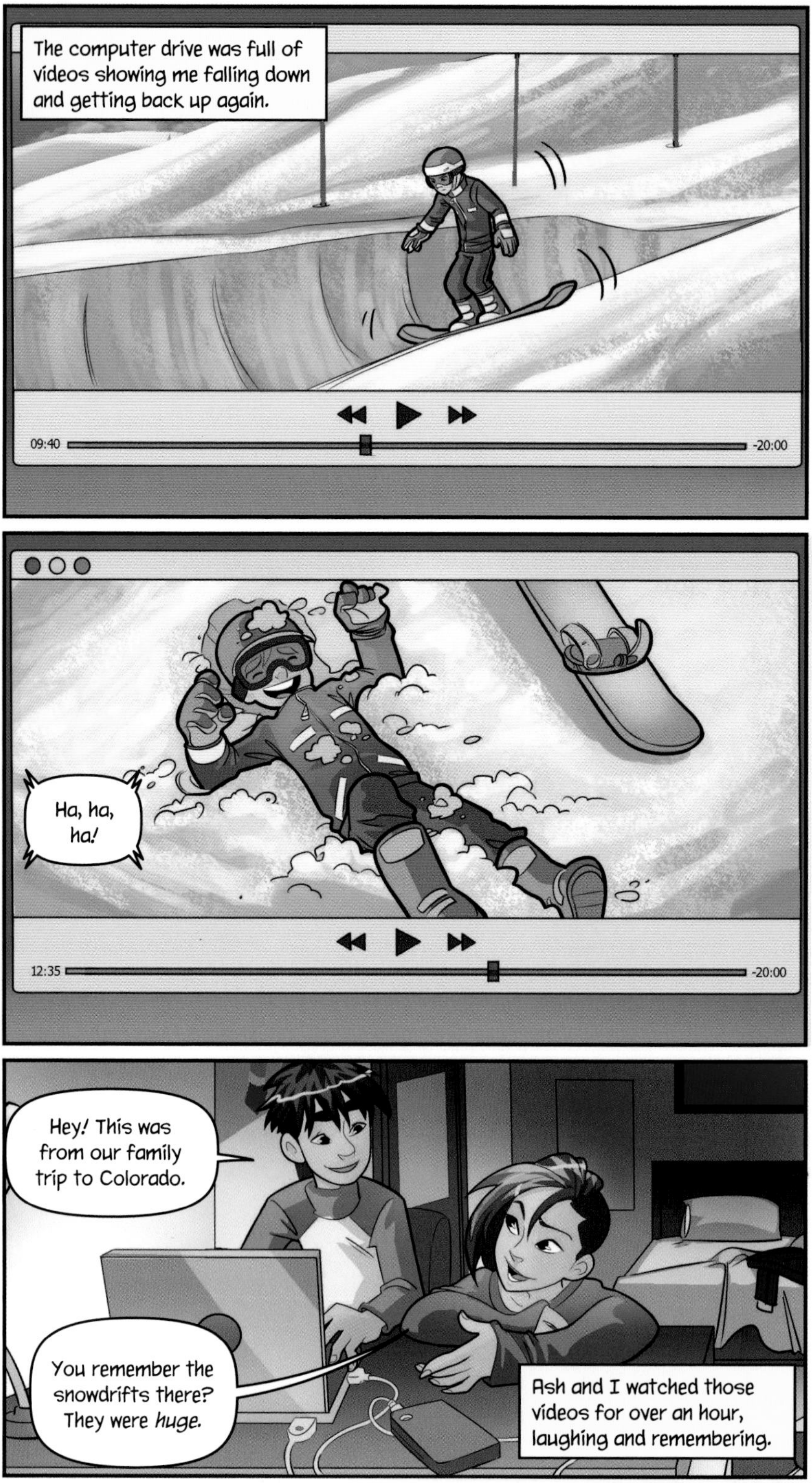
The computer drive was full of videos showing me falling down and getting back up again.
09:40
-20:00
Ha, ha, ha!
12:35
-20:00
Hey! This was from our family trip to Colorado.
You remember the snowdrifts there? They were *huge*.
Ash and I watched those videos for over an hour, laughing and remembering.

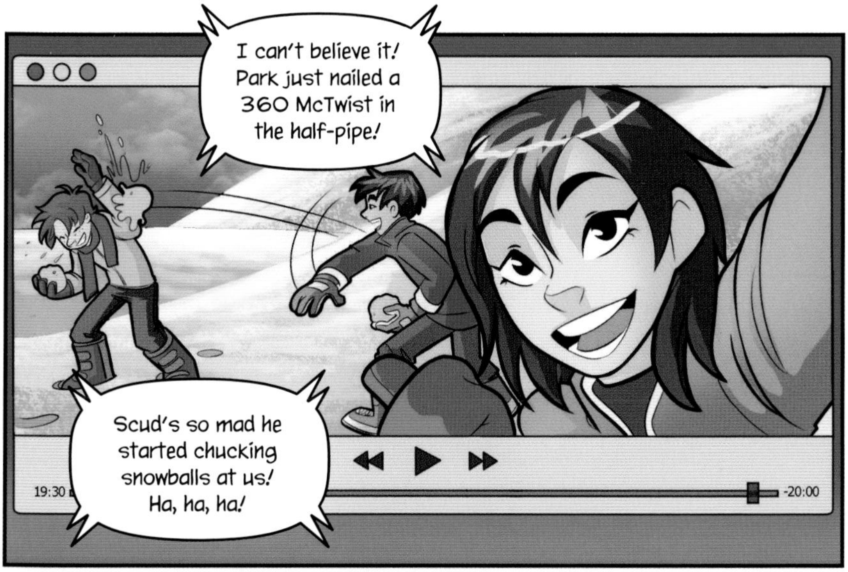
I can't believe it! Park just nailed a 360 McTwist in the half-pipe!
Scud's so mad he started chucking snowballs at us! Ha, ha, ha!
19:30
-20:00

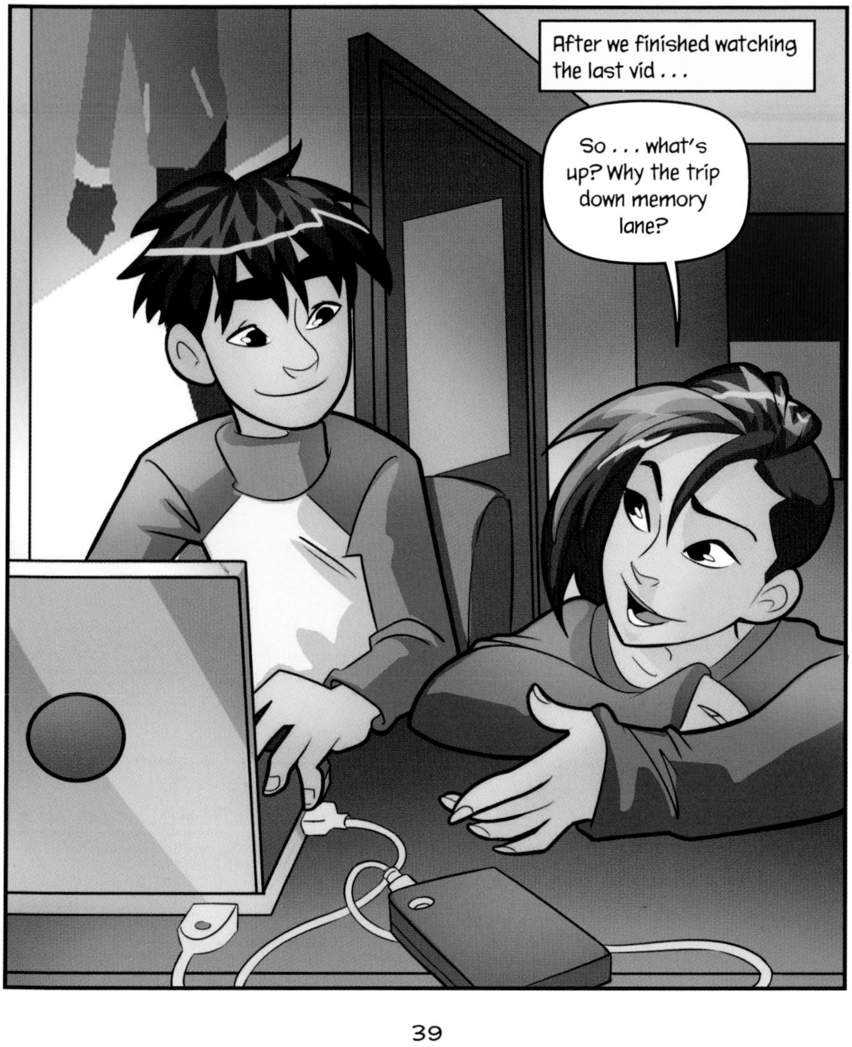
After we finished watching the last vid . . .
So . . . what's up? Why the trip down memory lane?

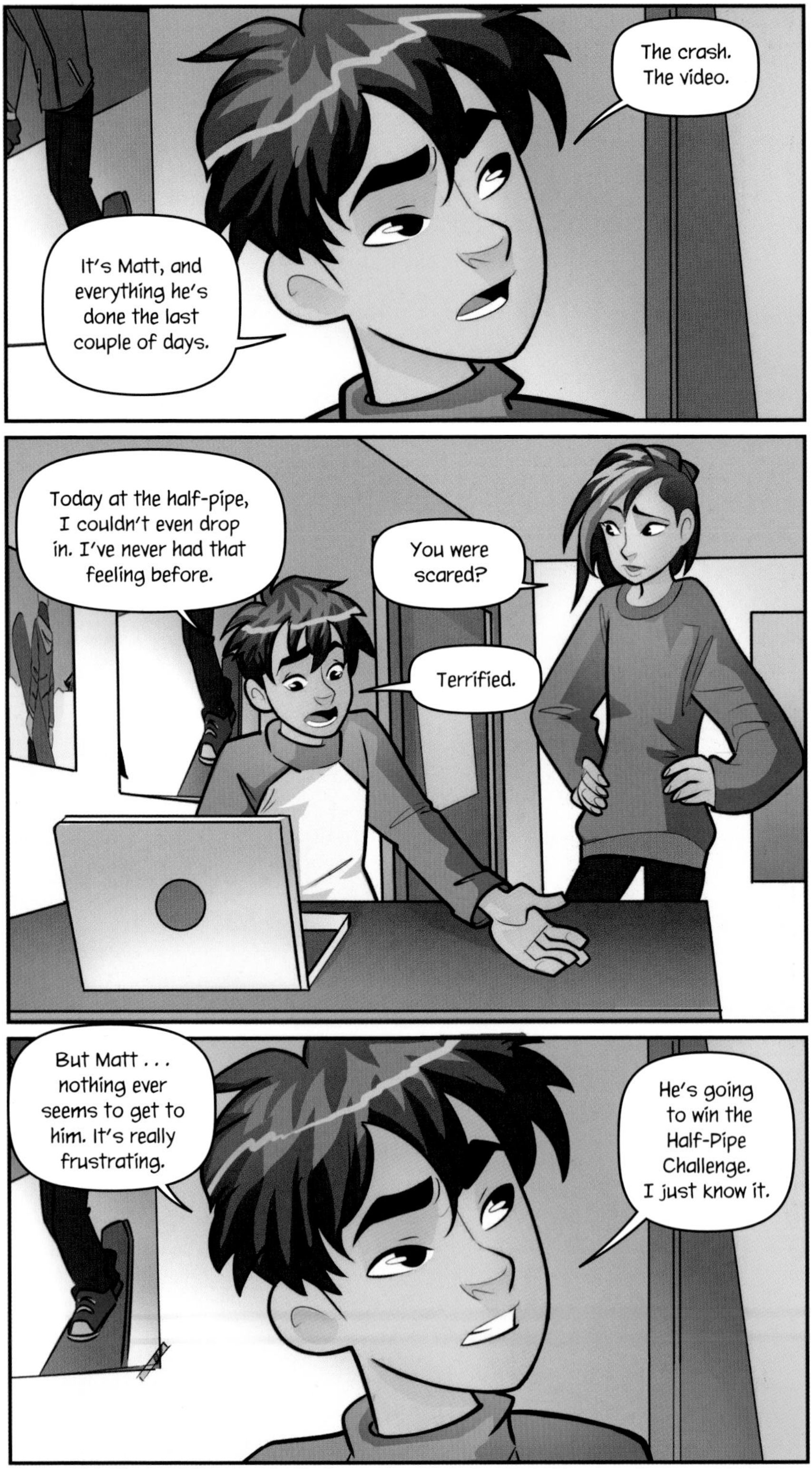
The crash. The video.
It's Matt, and everything he's done the last couple of days.
Today at the half-pipe, I couldn't even drop in. I've never had that feeling before.
You were scared?
Terrified.
But Matt . . . nothing ever seems to get to him. It's really frustrating.
He's going to win the Half-Pipe Challenge. I just know it.

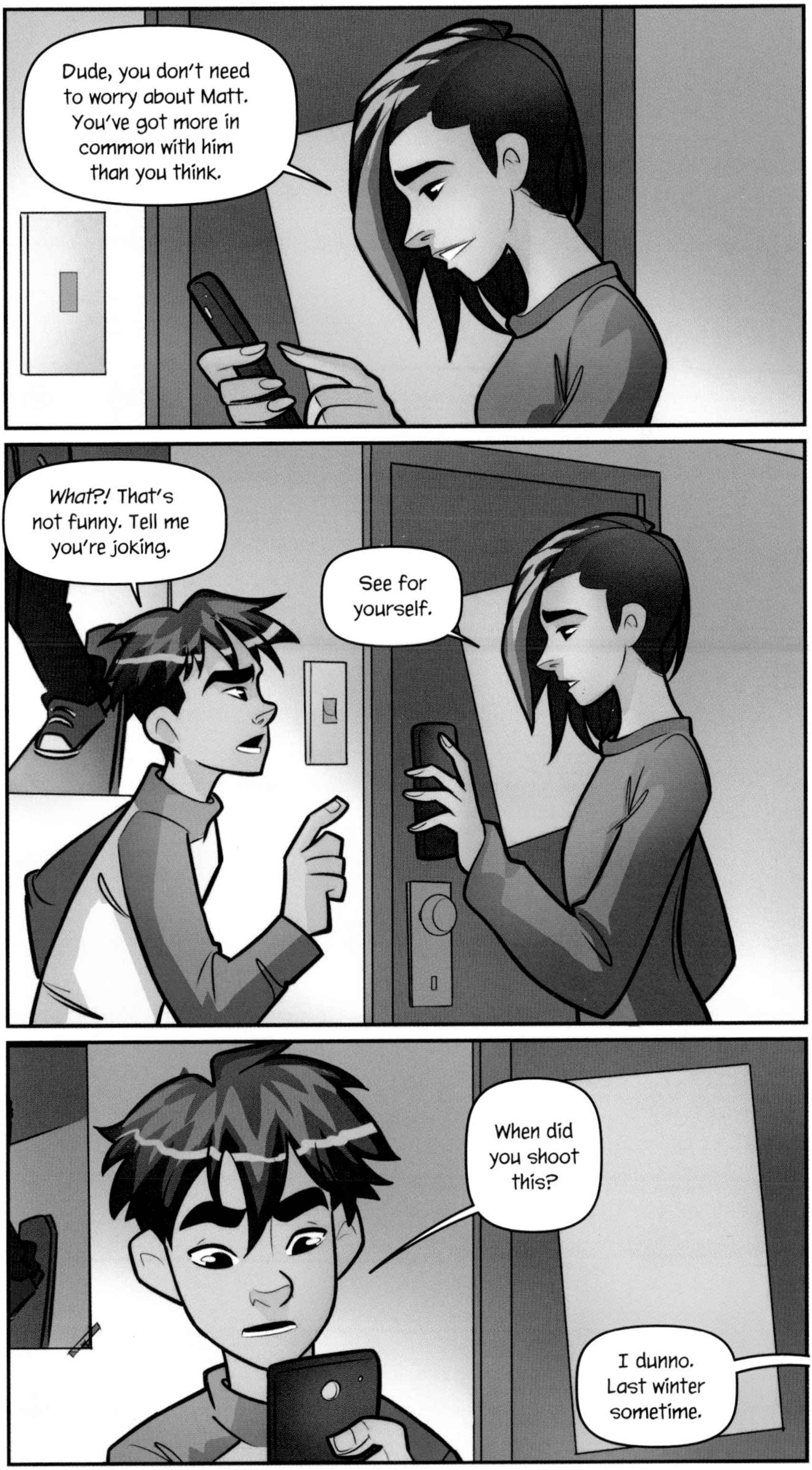
Dude, you don't need to worry about Matt. You've got more in common with him than you think.
What?! That's not funny. Tell me you're joking.
See for yourself.
When did you shoot this?
I dunno. Last winter sometime.

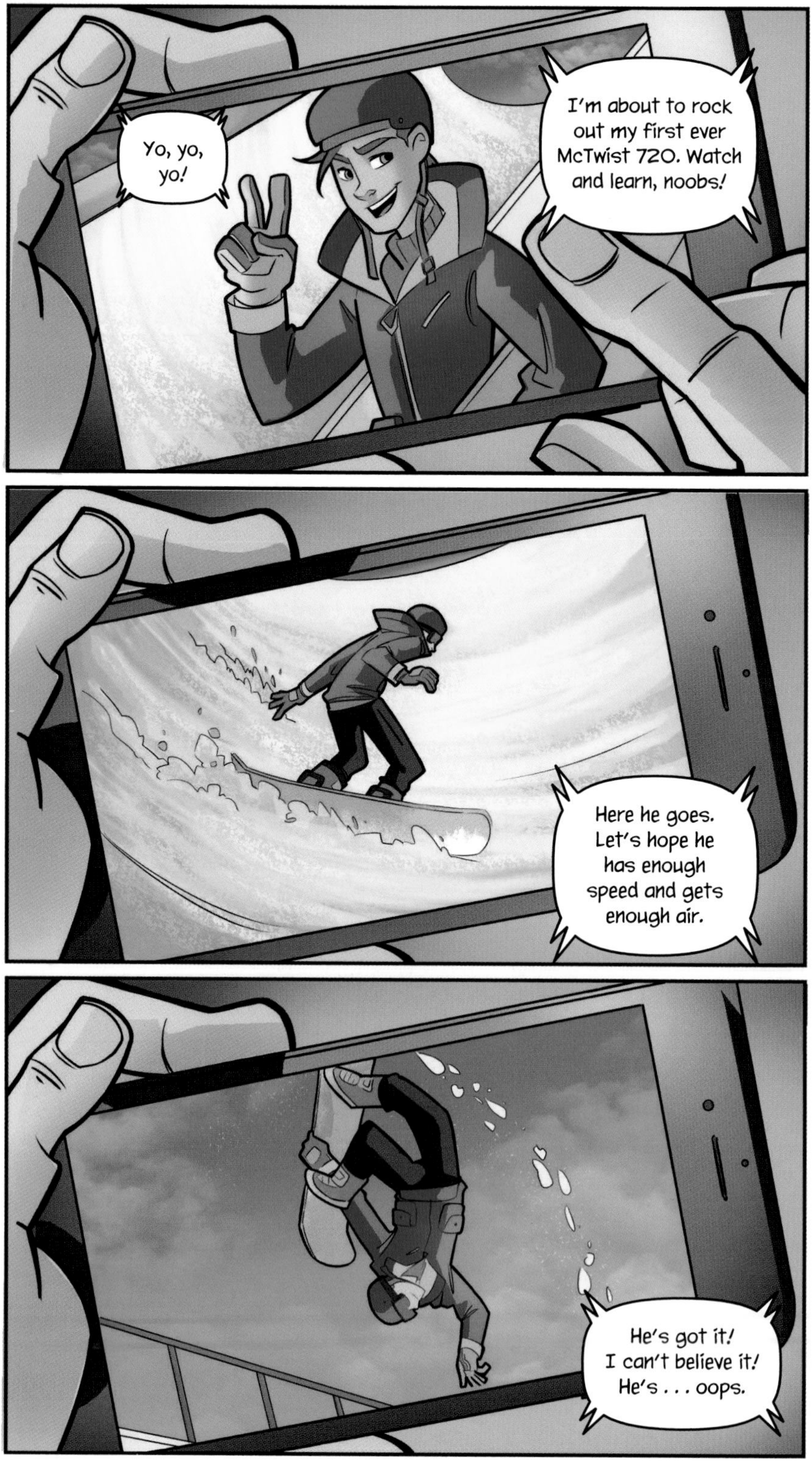
Yo, yo, yo!
I'm about to rock out my first ever McTwist 720. Watch and learn, noobs!
Here he goes. Let's hope he has enough speed and gets enough air.
He's got it! I can't believe it! He's . . . oops.

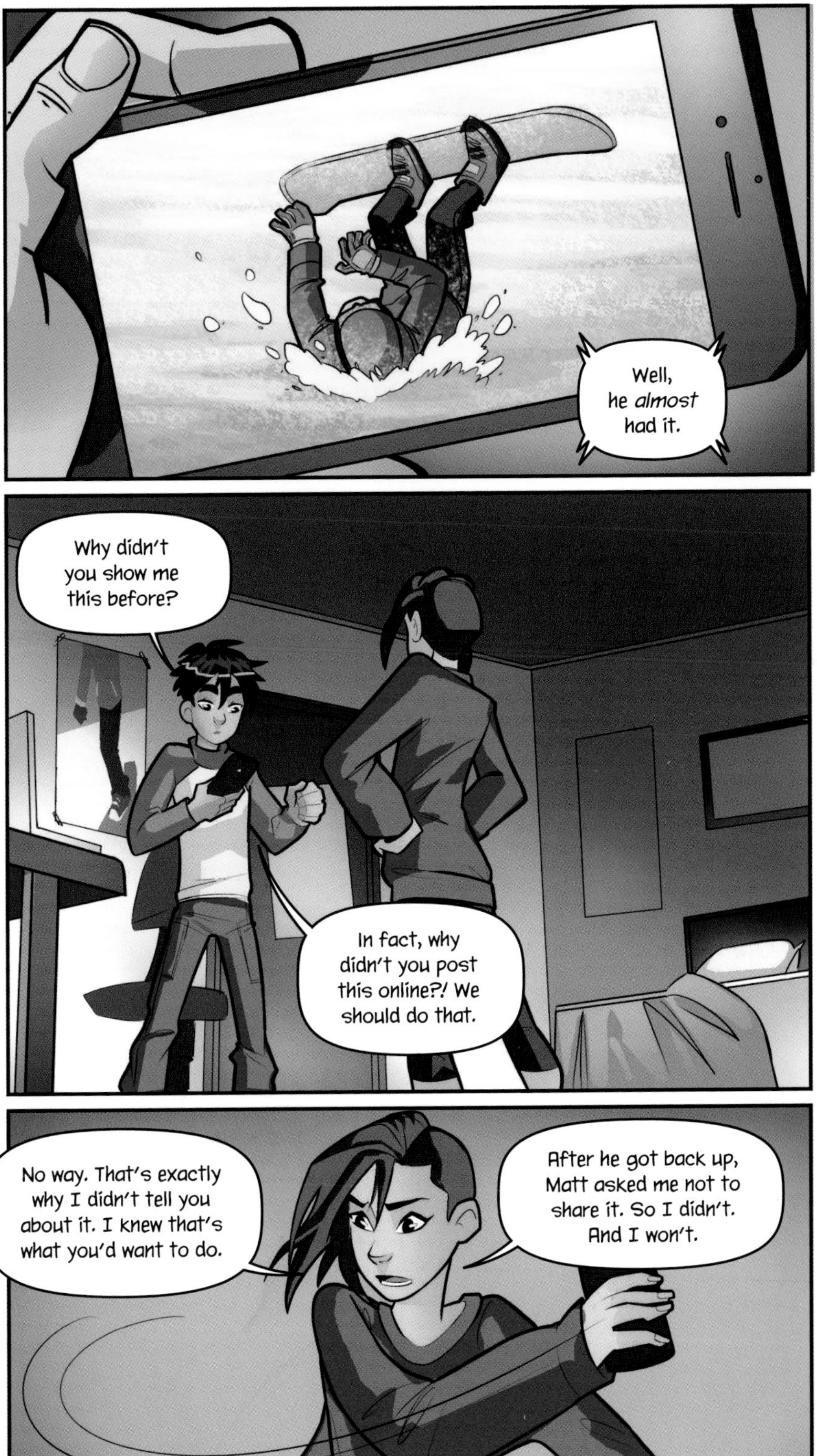
Well, he *almost* had it.
Why didn't you show me this before?
In fact, why didn't you post this online?! We should do that.
No way. That's exactly why I didn't tell you about it. I knew that's what you'd want to do.
After he got back up, Matt asked me not to share it. So I didn't. And I won't.

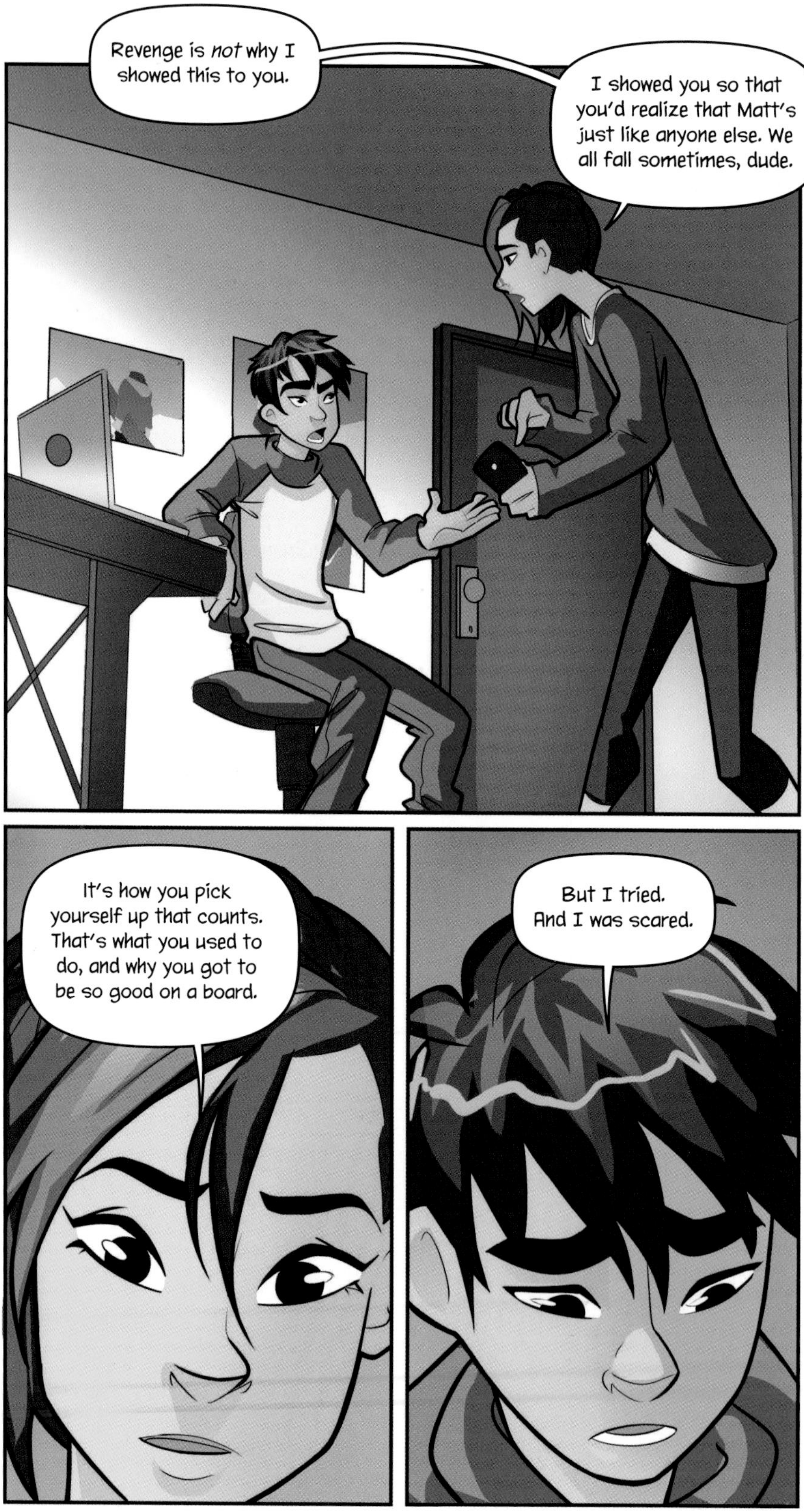
Revenge is *not* why I showed this to you.
I showed you so that you'd realize that Matt's just like anyone else. We all fall sometimes, dude.
It's how you pick yourself up that counts. That's what you used to do, and why you got to be so good on a board.
But I tried. And I was scared.

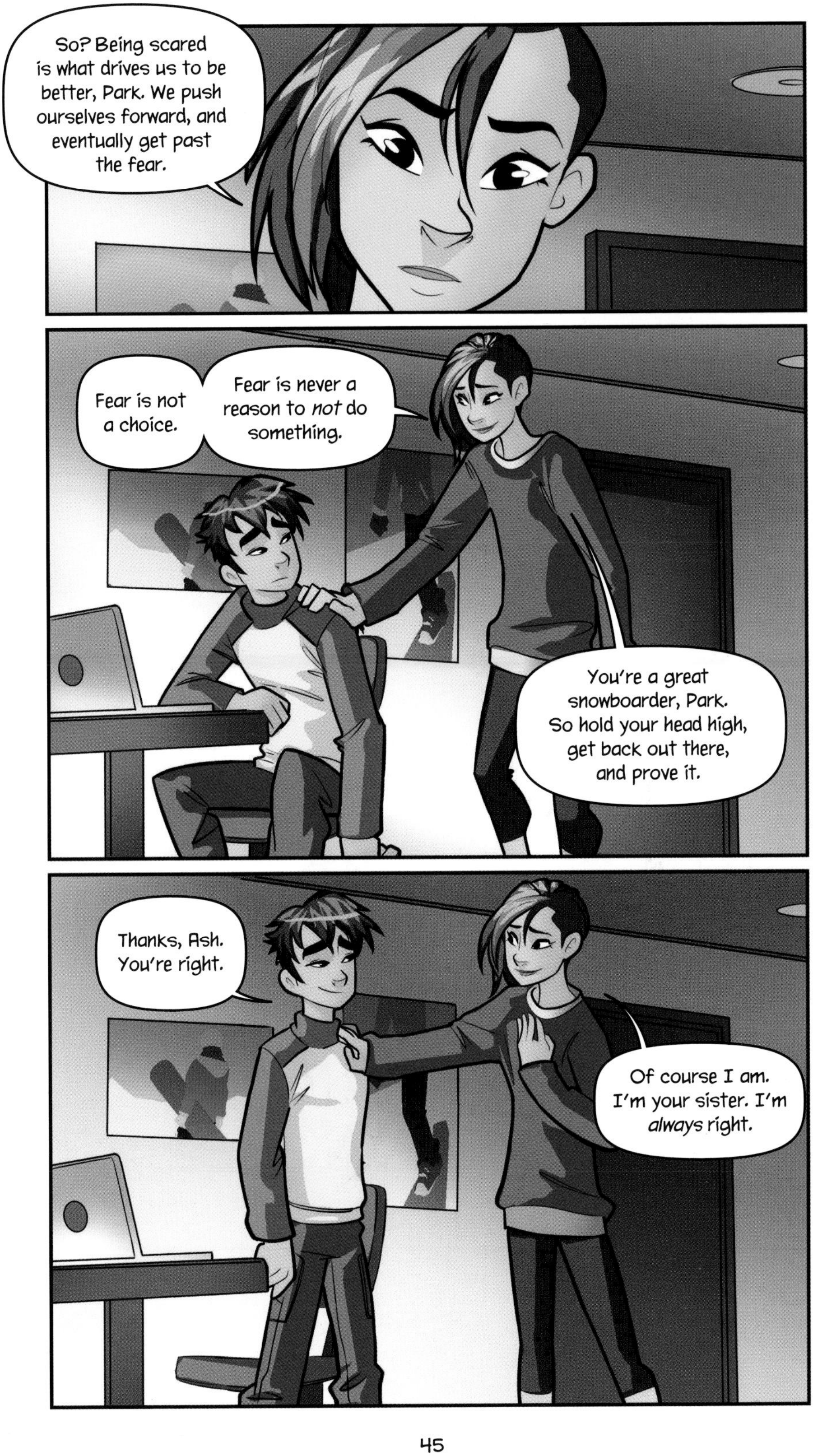
So? Being scared is what drives us to be better, Park. We push ourselves forward, and eventually get past the fear.
Fear is not a choice.
Fear is never a reason to *not* do something.
You're a great snowboarder, Park. So hold your head high, get back out there, and prove it.
Thanks, Ash. You're right.
Of course I am. I'm your sister. I'm *always* right.

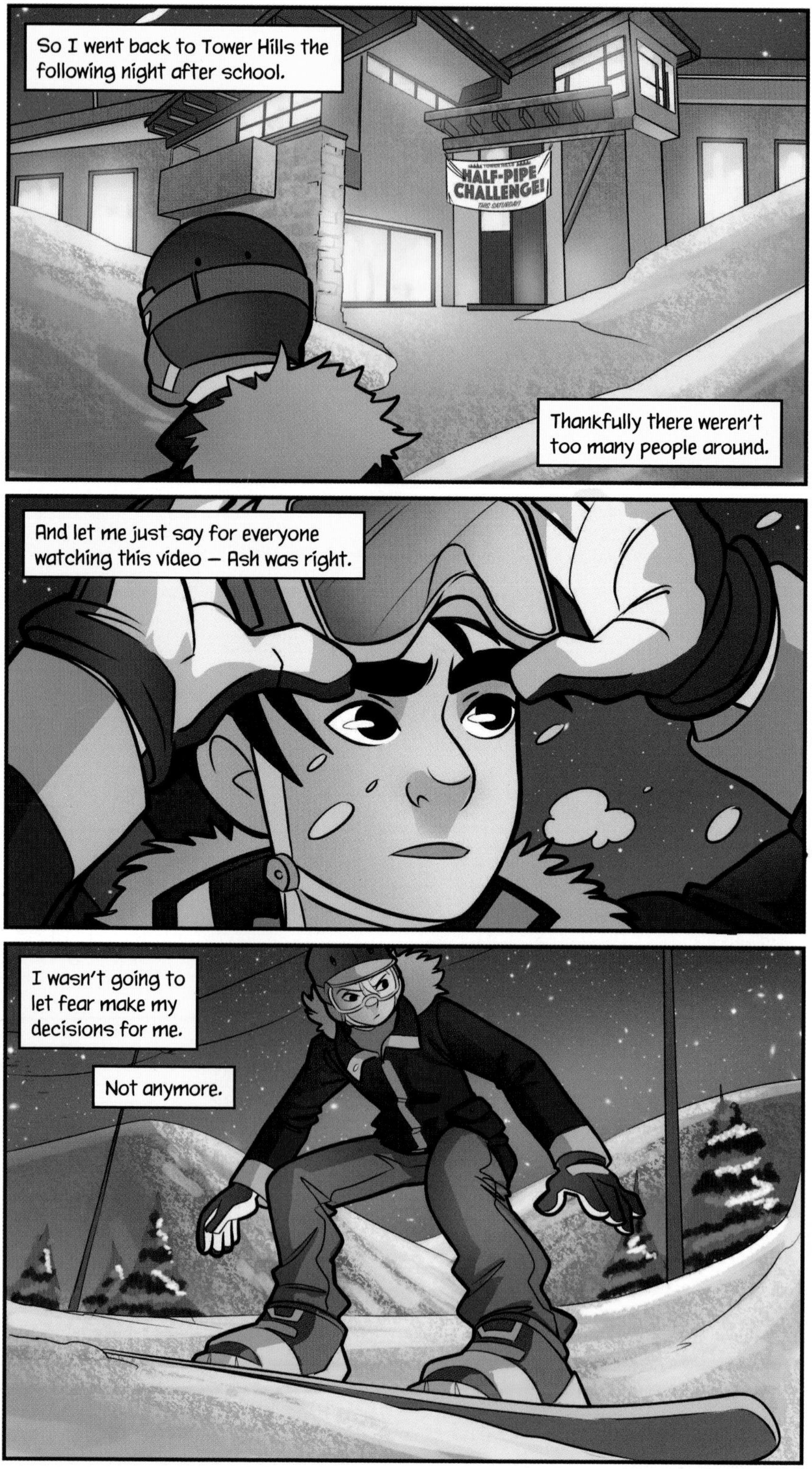
So I went back to Tower Hills the following night after school.
HALF-PIPE CHALLENGE!
Thankfully there weren't too many people around.
And let me just say for everyone watching this video — Ash was right.
I wasn't going to let fear make my decisions for me.
Not anymore.

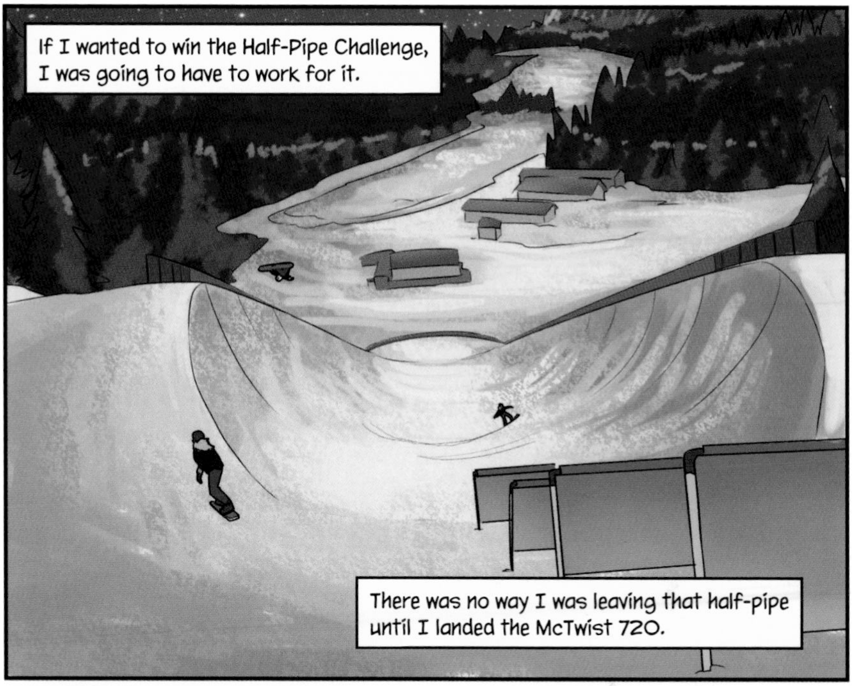
If I wanted to win the Half-Pipe Challenge, I was going to have to work for it.
There was no way I was leaving that half-pipe until I landed the McTwist 720.

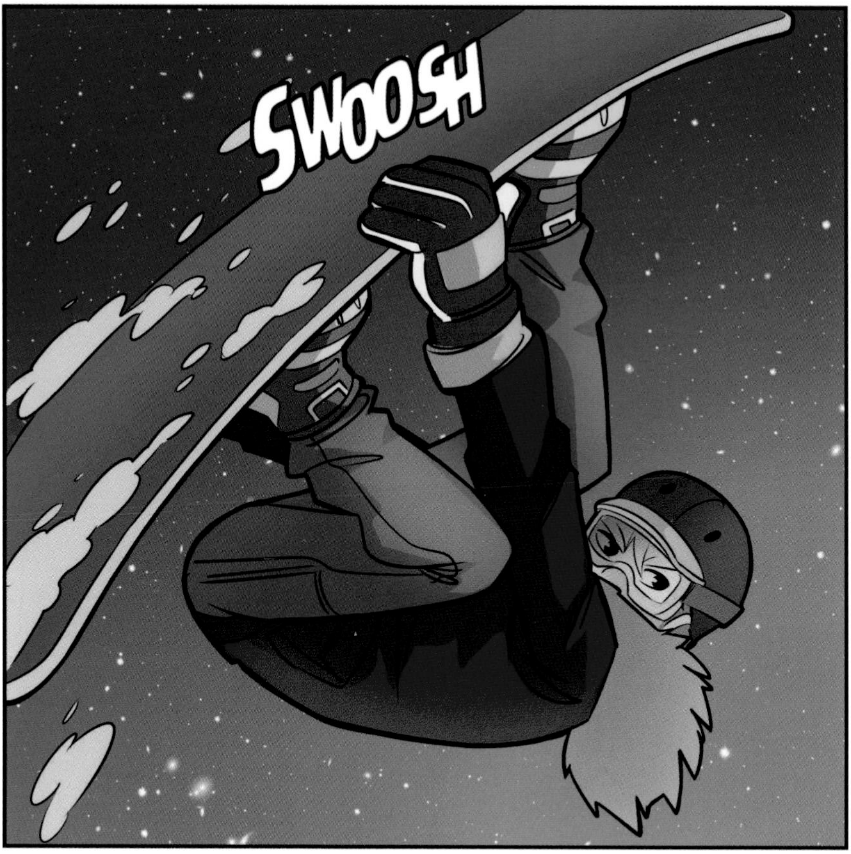
SWOOSH

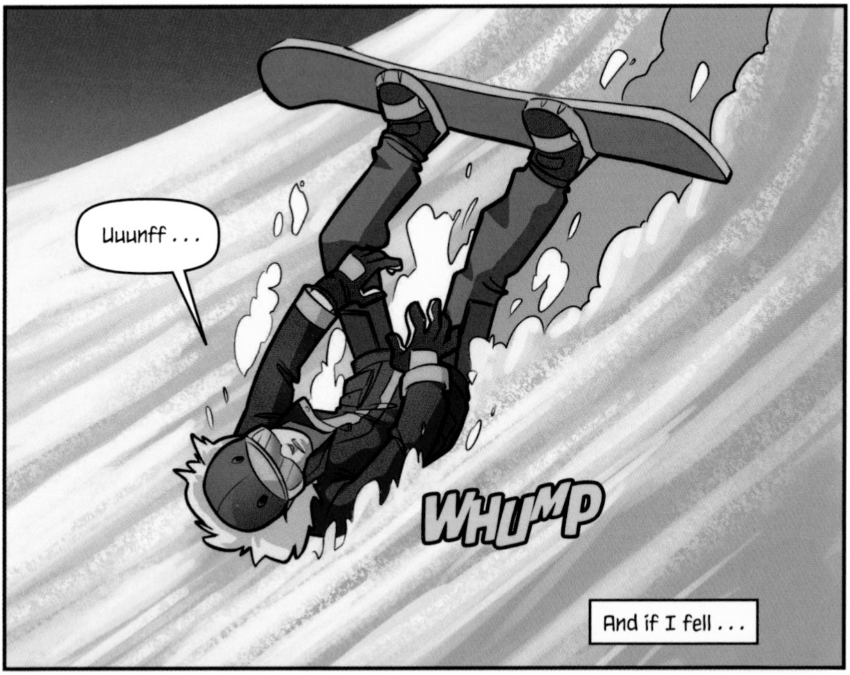
Uuunff . . .
WHUMP
And if I fell . . .

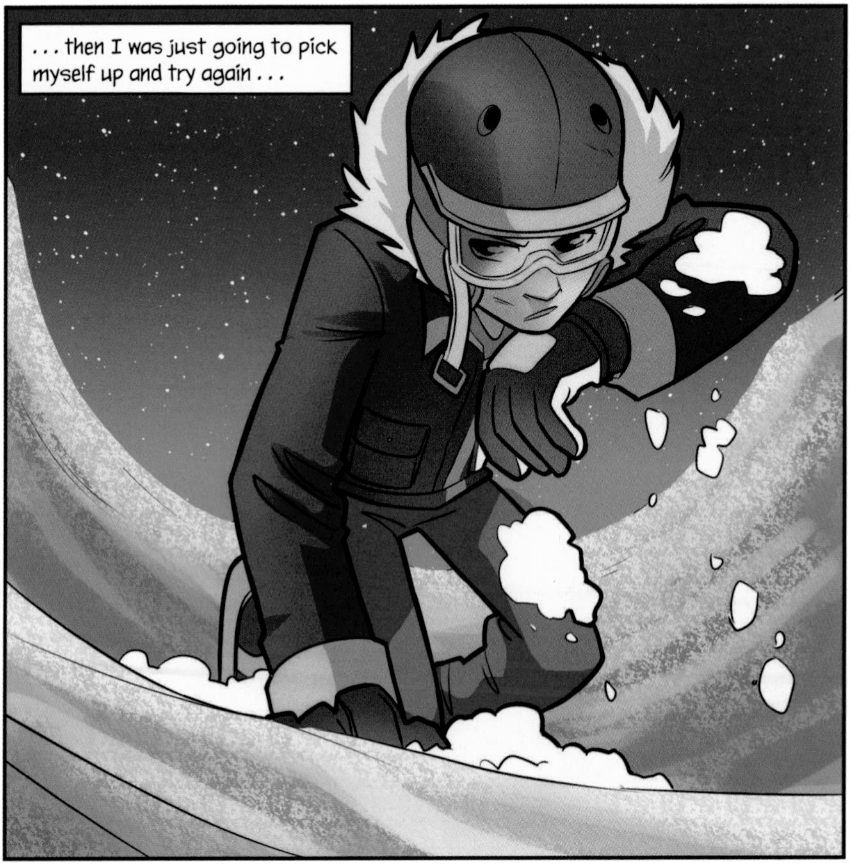
. . . then I was just going to pick myself up and try again . . .

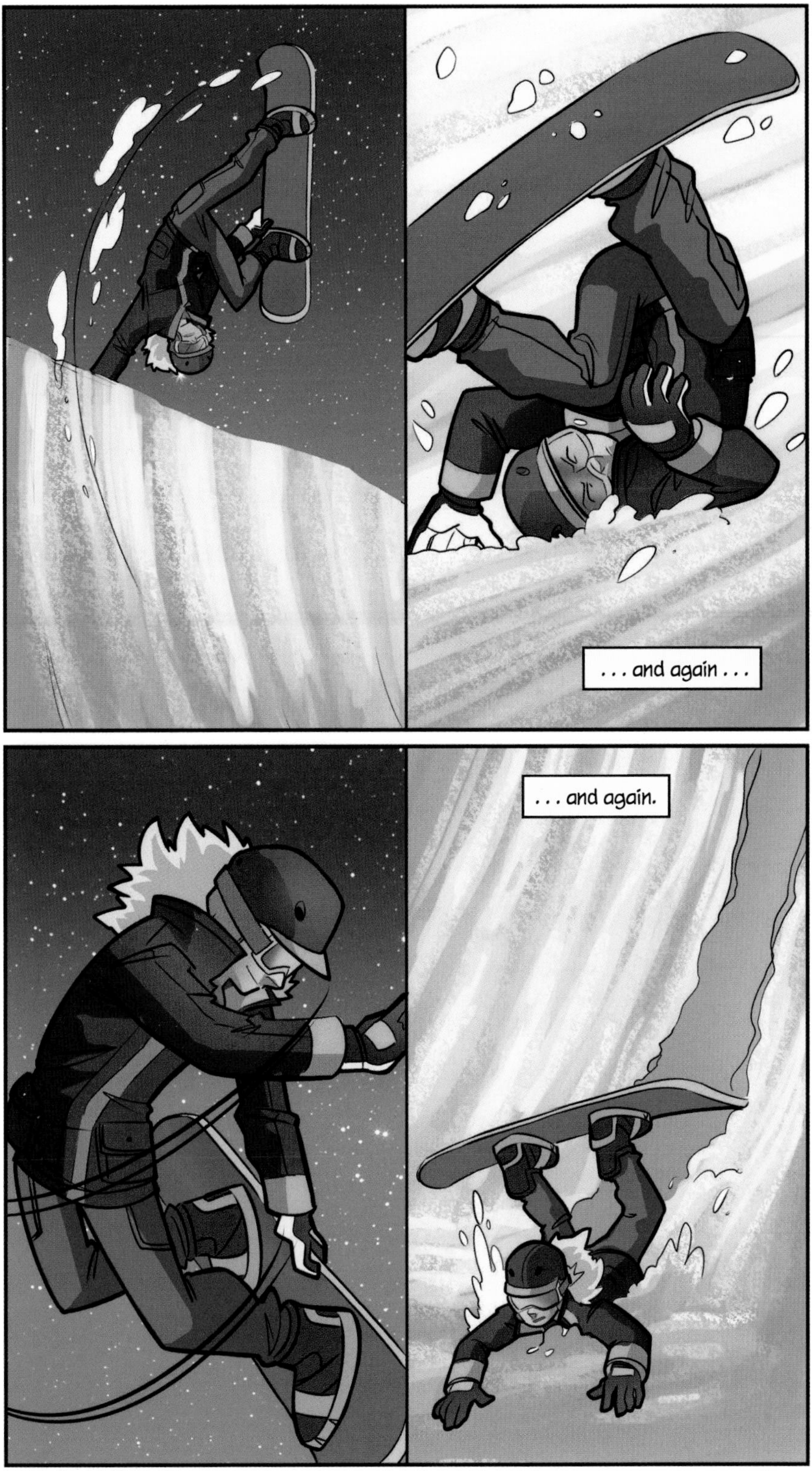
. . . and again . . .
. . . and again.

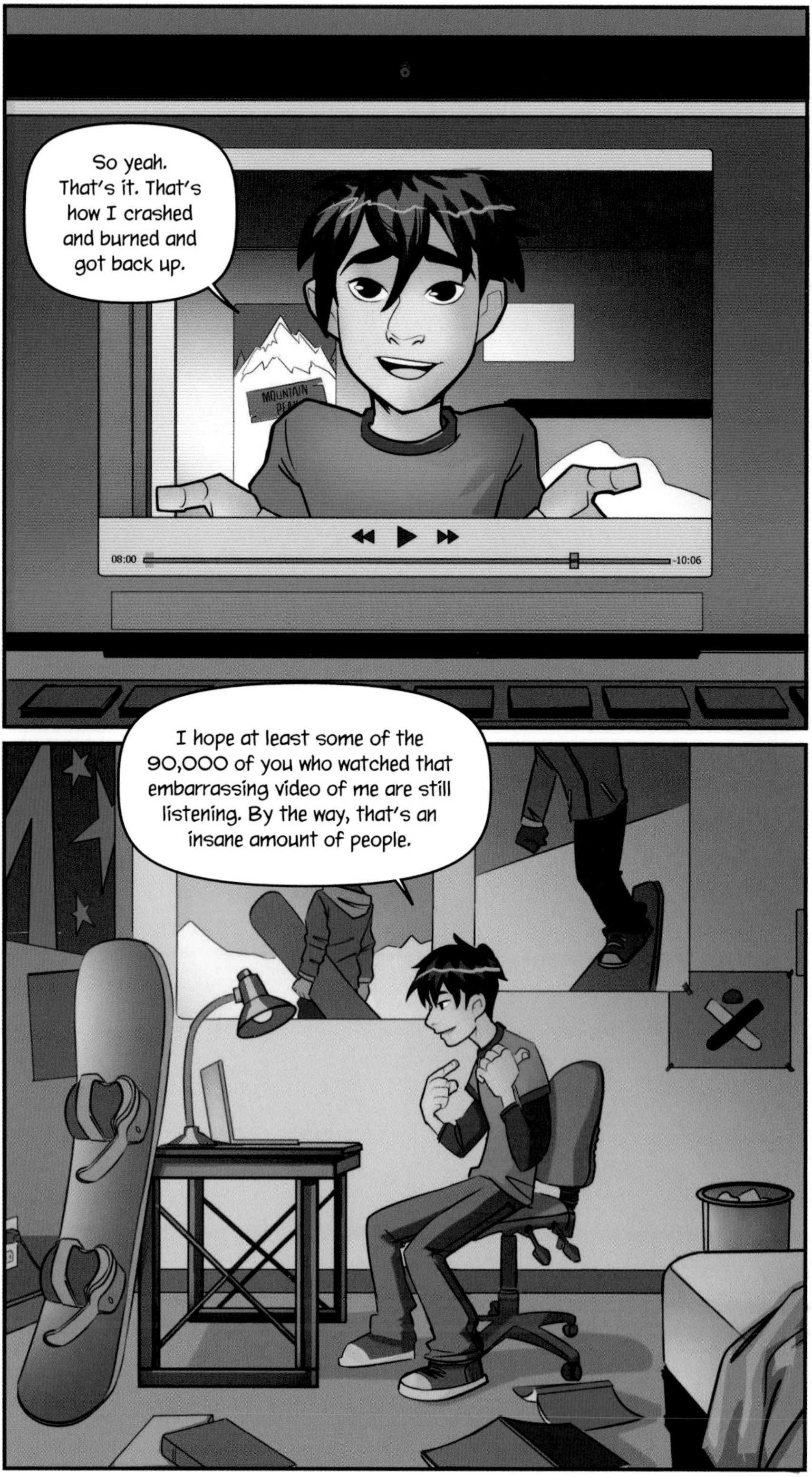
So yeah. That's it. That's how I crashed and burned and got back up.
MOUNTAIN PEAK
08:00
-10:06
I hope at least some of the 90,000 of you who watched that embarrassing video of me are still listening. By the way, that's an insane amount of people.

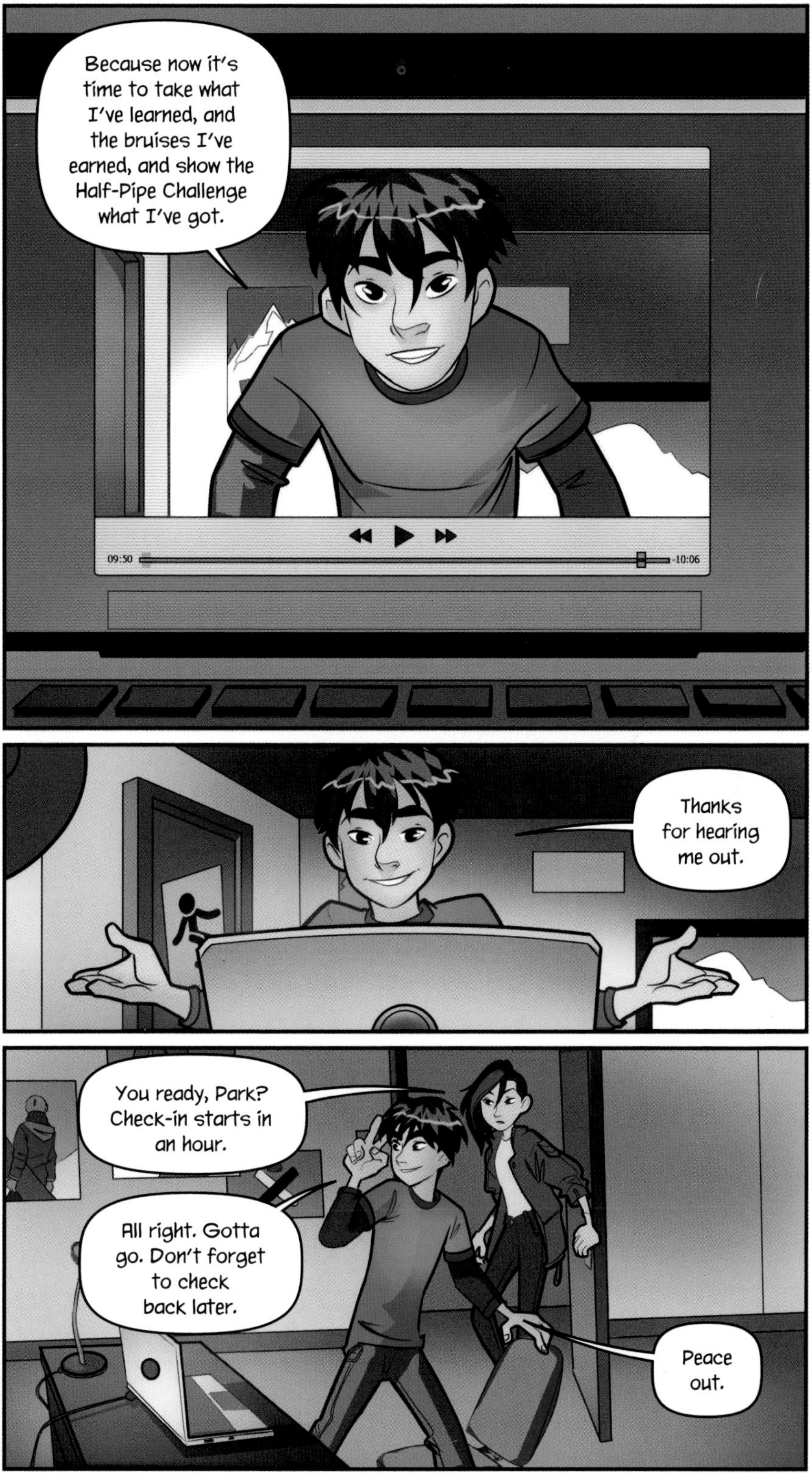
Because now it's time to take what I've learned, and the bruises I've earned, and show the Half-Pipe Challenge what I've got.
09:50
-10:06
Thanks for hearing me out.
You ready, Park? Check-in starts in an hour.
All right. Gotta go. Don't forget to check back later.
Peace out.

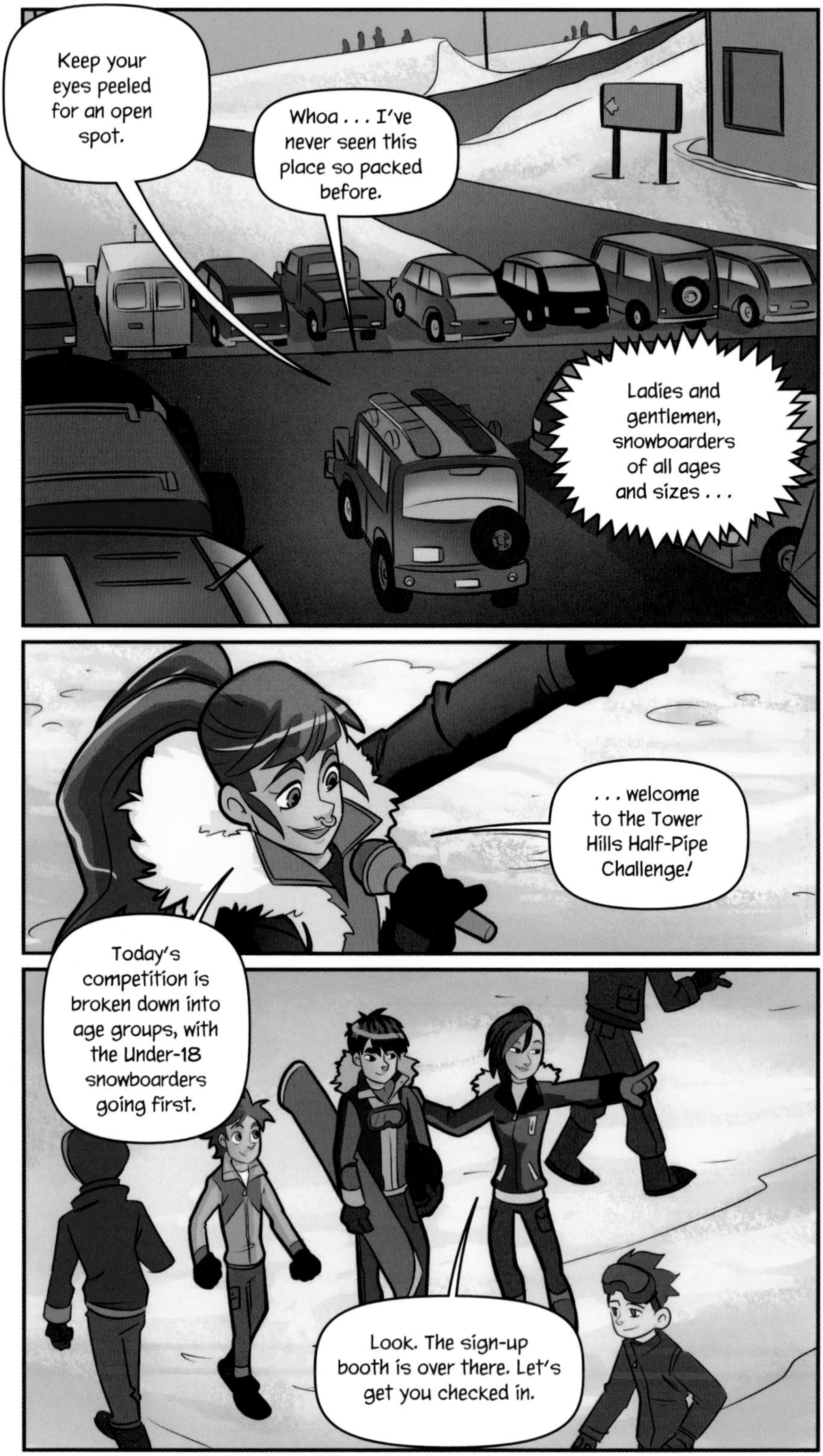
Keep your eyes peeled for an open spot.
Whoa . . . I've never seen this place so packed before.
Ladies and gentlemen, snowboarders of all ages and sizes . . .
. . . welcome to the Tower Hills Half-Pipe Challenge!
Today's competition is broken down into age groups, with the Under-18 snowboarders going first.
Look. The sign-up booth is over there. Let's get you checked in.

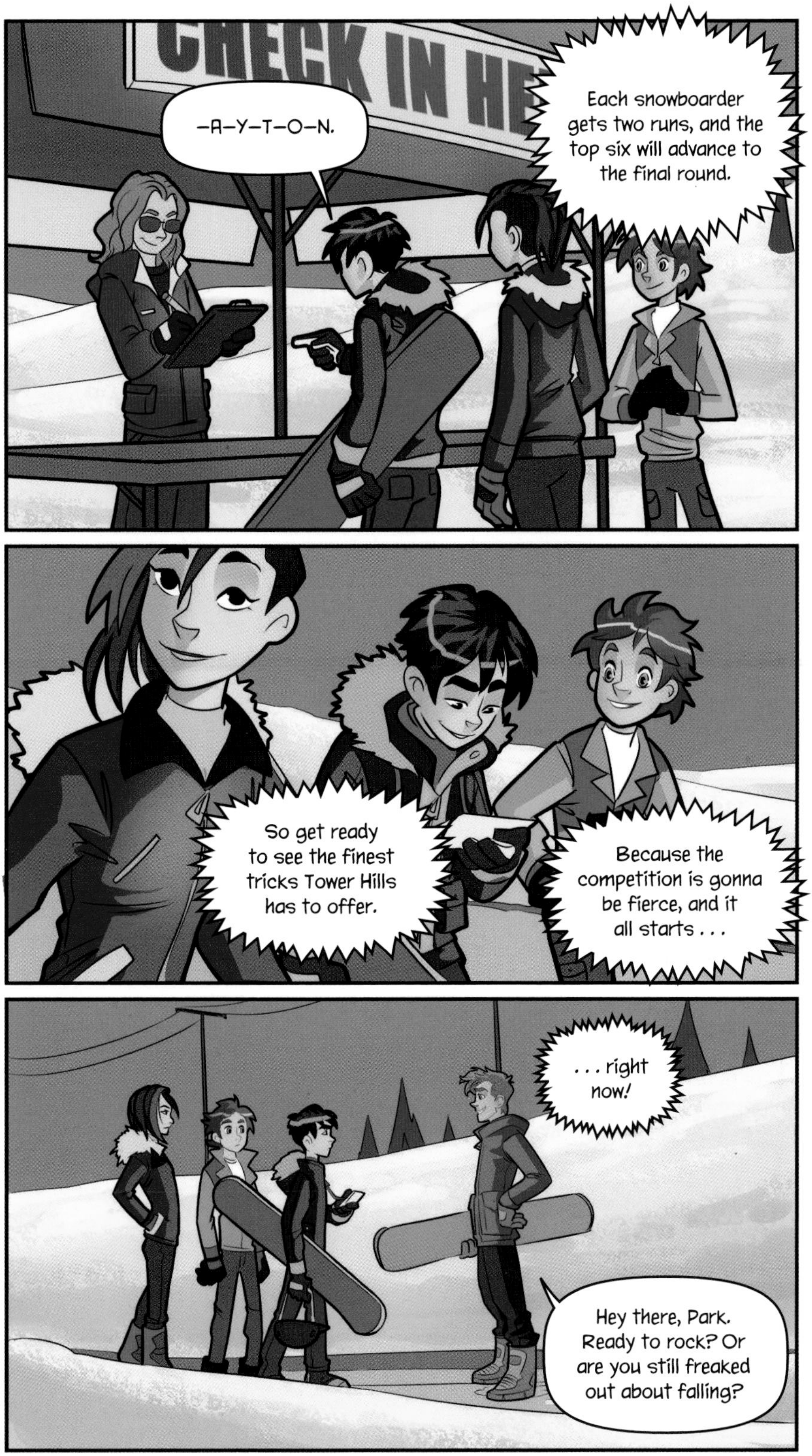
CHECK IN HE
-A-Y-T-O-N.
Each snowboarder gets two runs, and the top six will advance to the final round.
So get ready to see the finest tricks Tower Hills has to offer.
Because the competition is gonna be fierce, and it all starts . . .
. . . right now!
Hey there, Park. Ready to rock? Or are you still freaked out about falling?

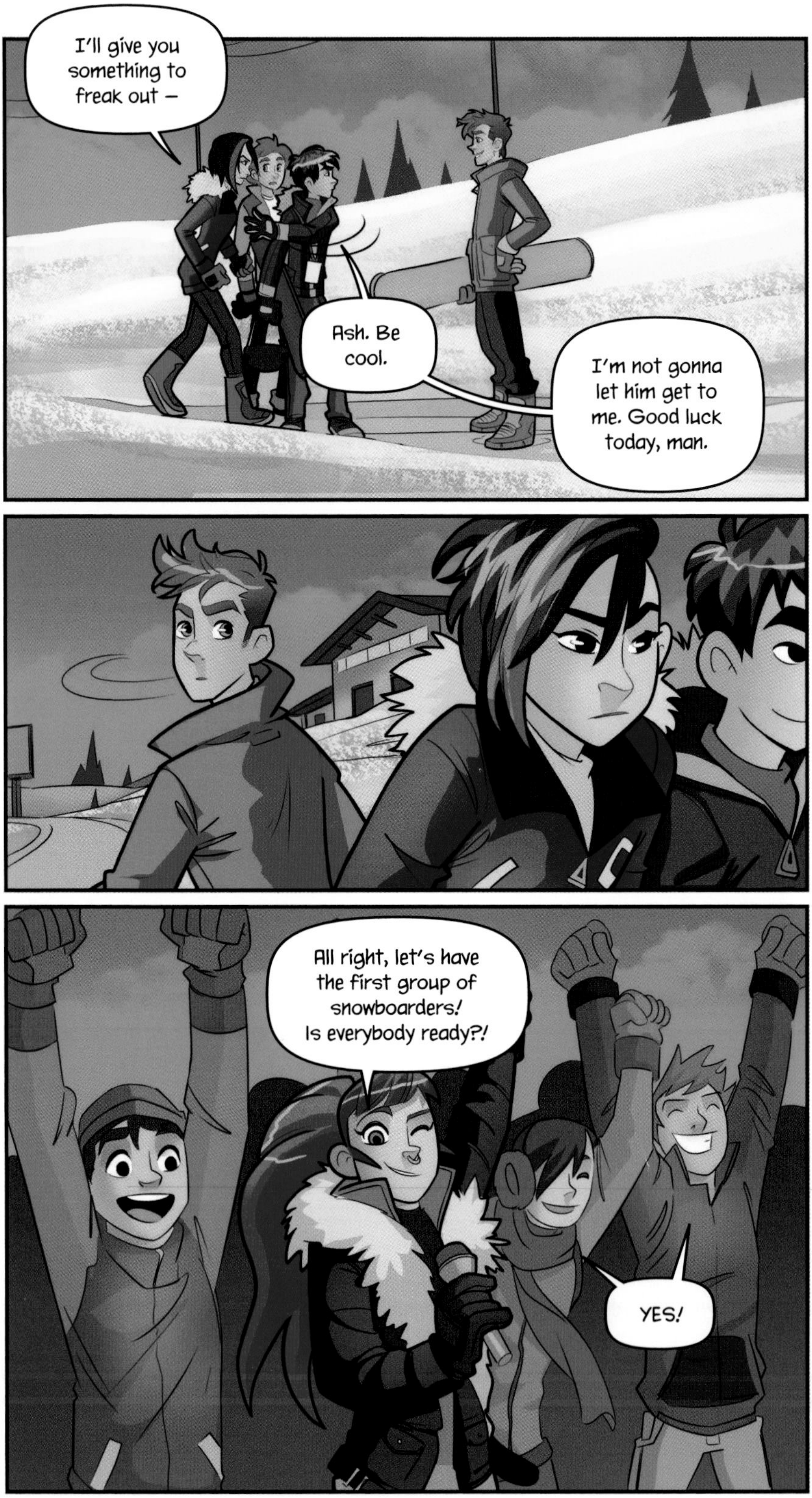
I'll give you something to freak out –
Ash. Be cool.
I'm not gonna let him get to me. Good luck today, man.
All right, let's have the first group of snowboarders! Is everybody ready?!
YES!

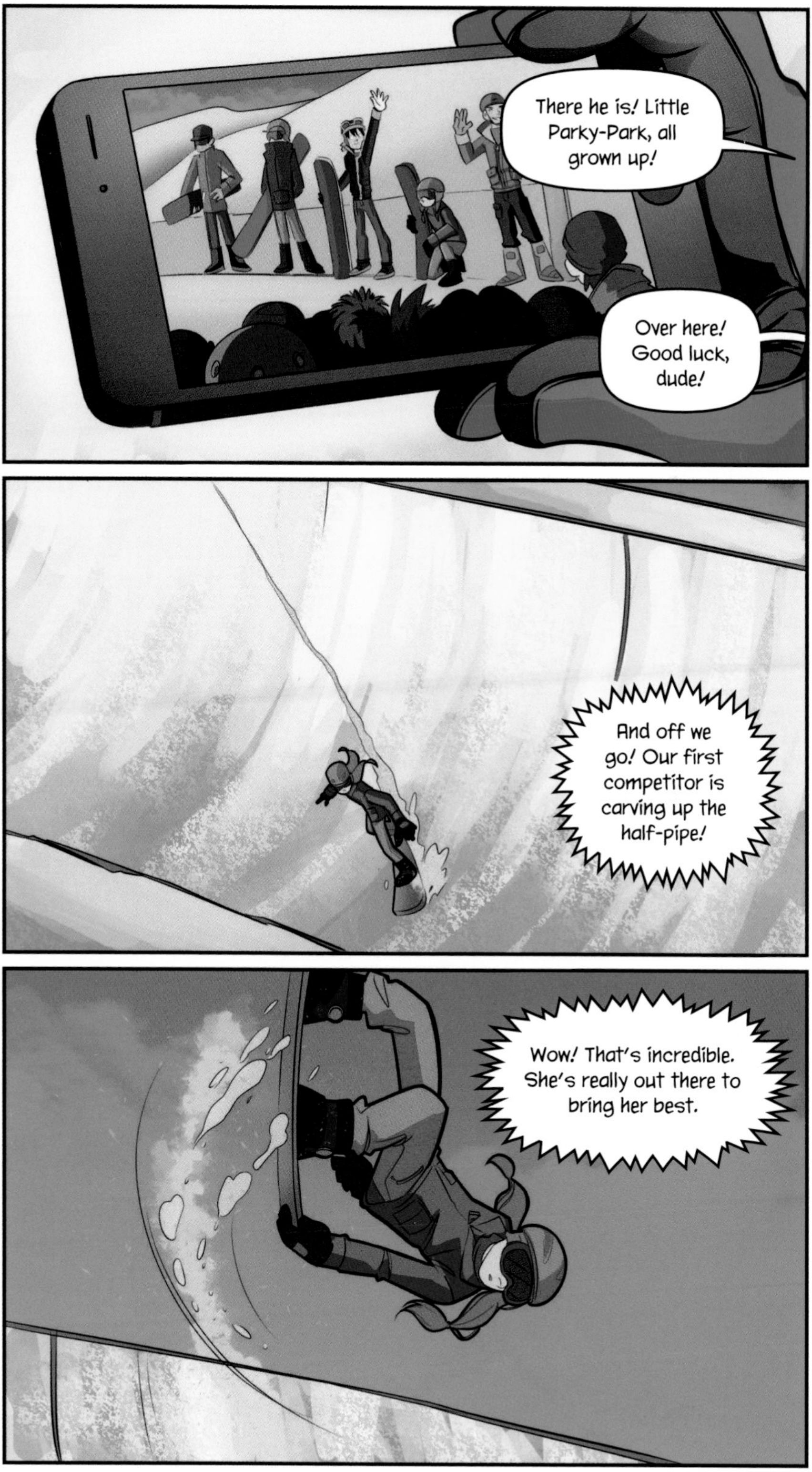
There he is! Little Parky-Park, all grown up!
Over here! Good luck, dude!
And off we go! Our first competitor is carving up the half-pipe!
Wow! That's incredible. She's really out there to bring her best.

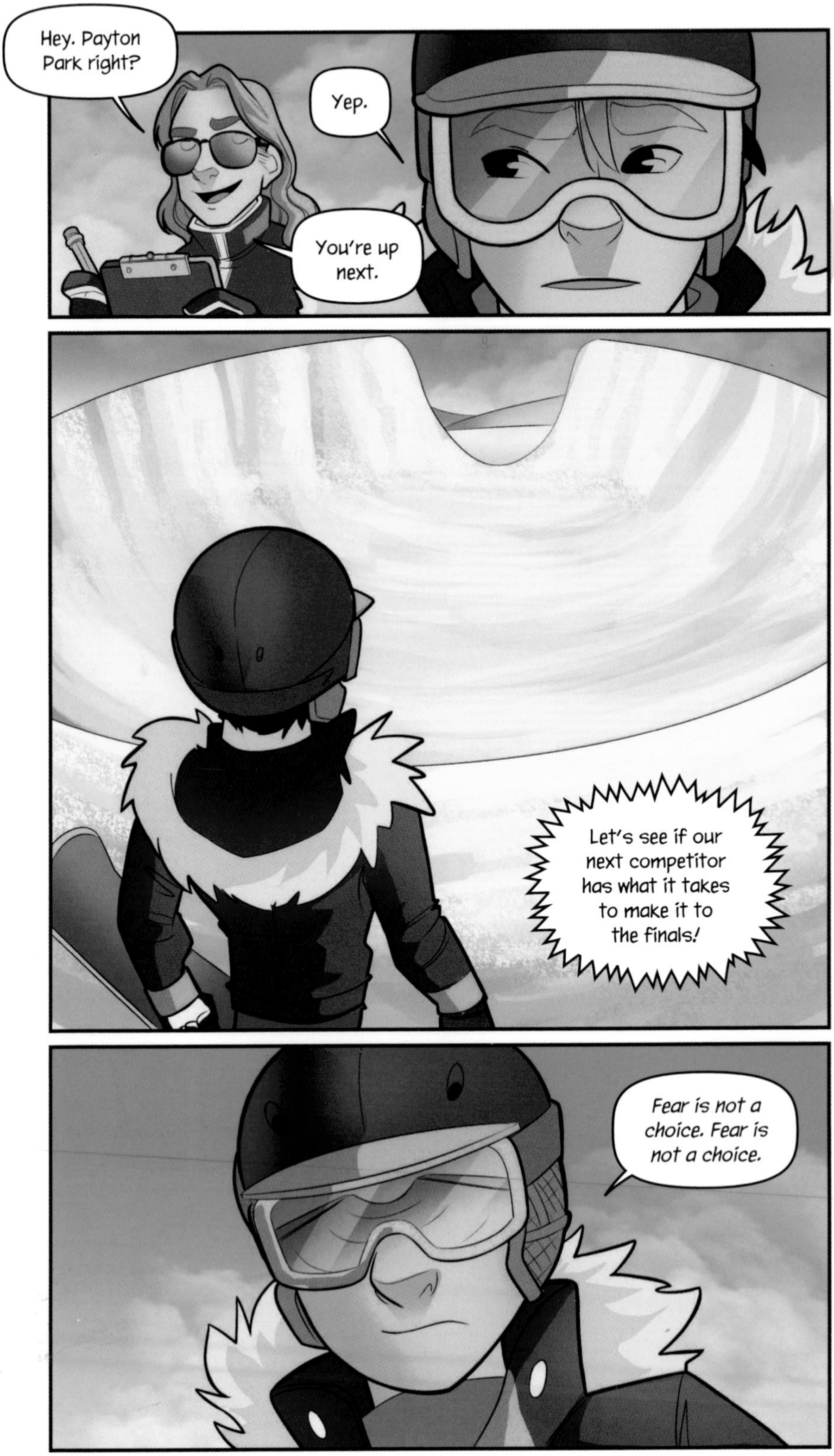
Hey. Payton Park right?
Yep.
You're up next.
Let's see if our next competitor has what it takes to make it to the finals!
Fear is not a choice. Fear is not a choice.

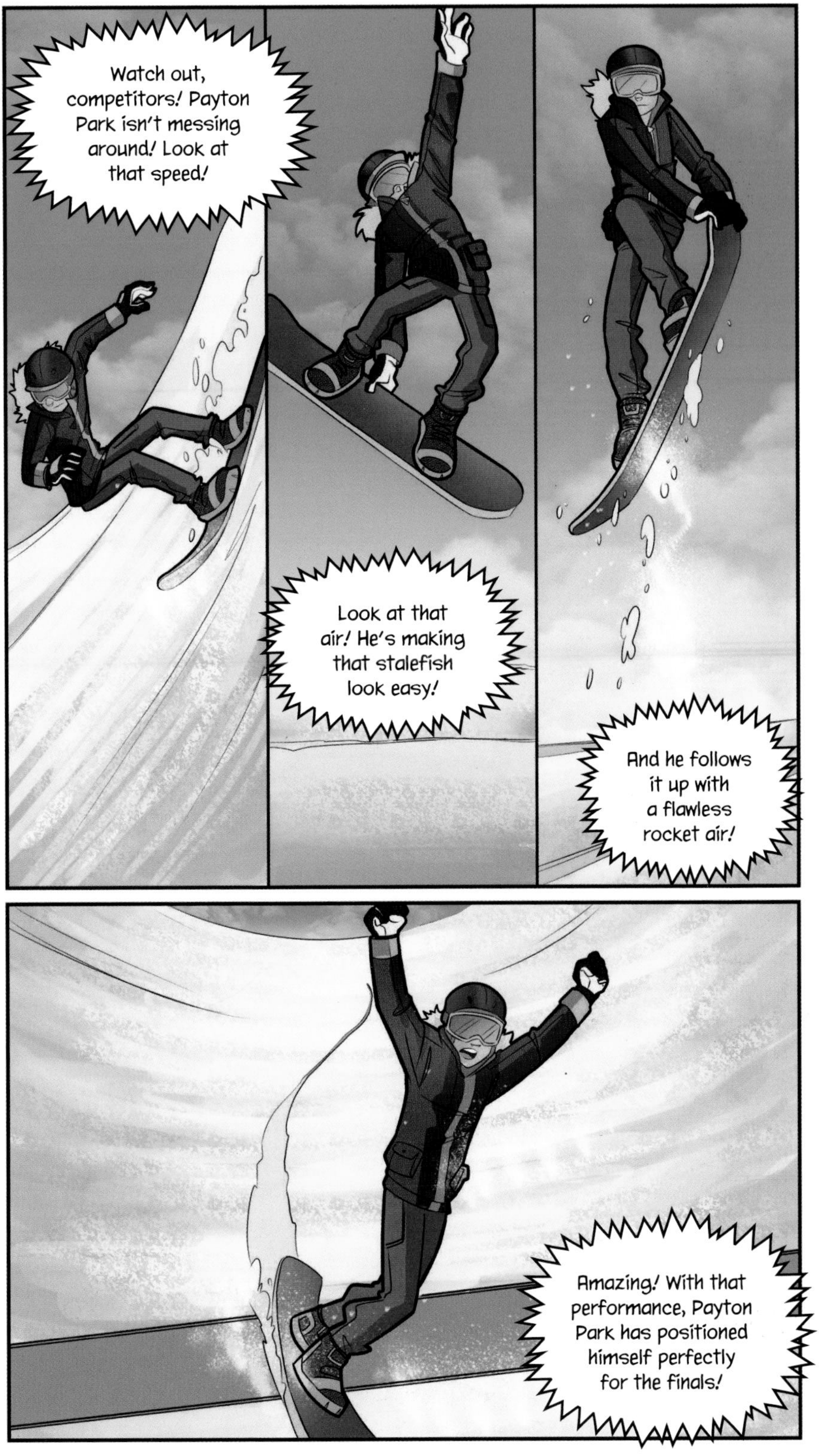
Watch out, competitors! Payton Park isn't messing around! Look at that speed!
Look at that air! He's making that stalefish look easy!
And he follows it up with a flawless rocket air!
Amazing! With that performance, Payton Park has positioned himself perfectly for the finals!

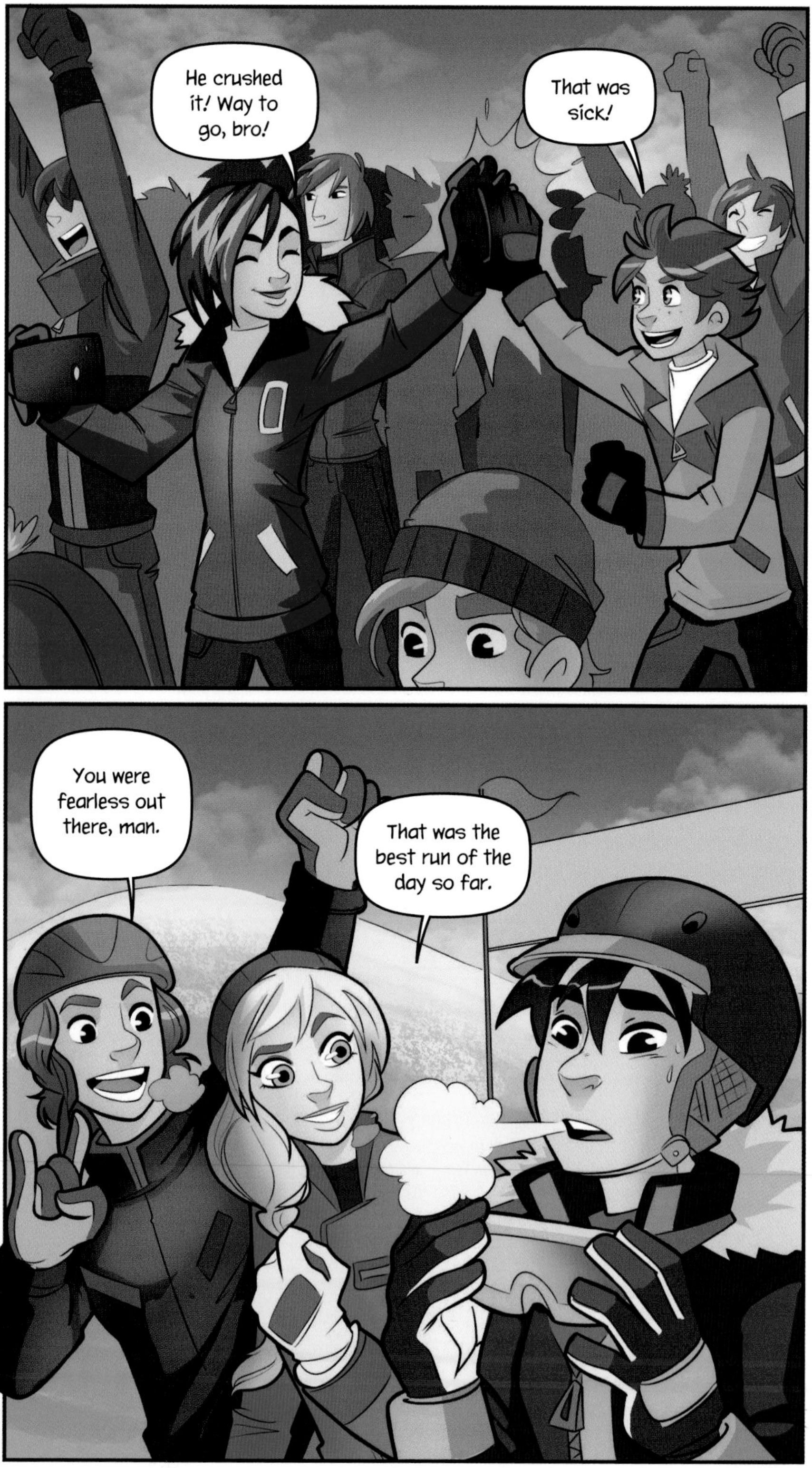
He crushed it! Way to go, bro!
That was sick!
You were fearless out there, man.
That was the best run of the day so far.

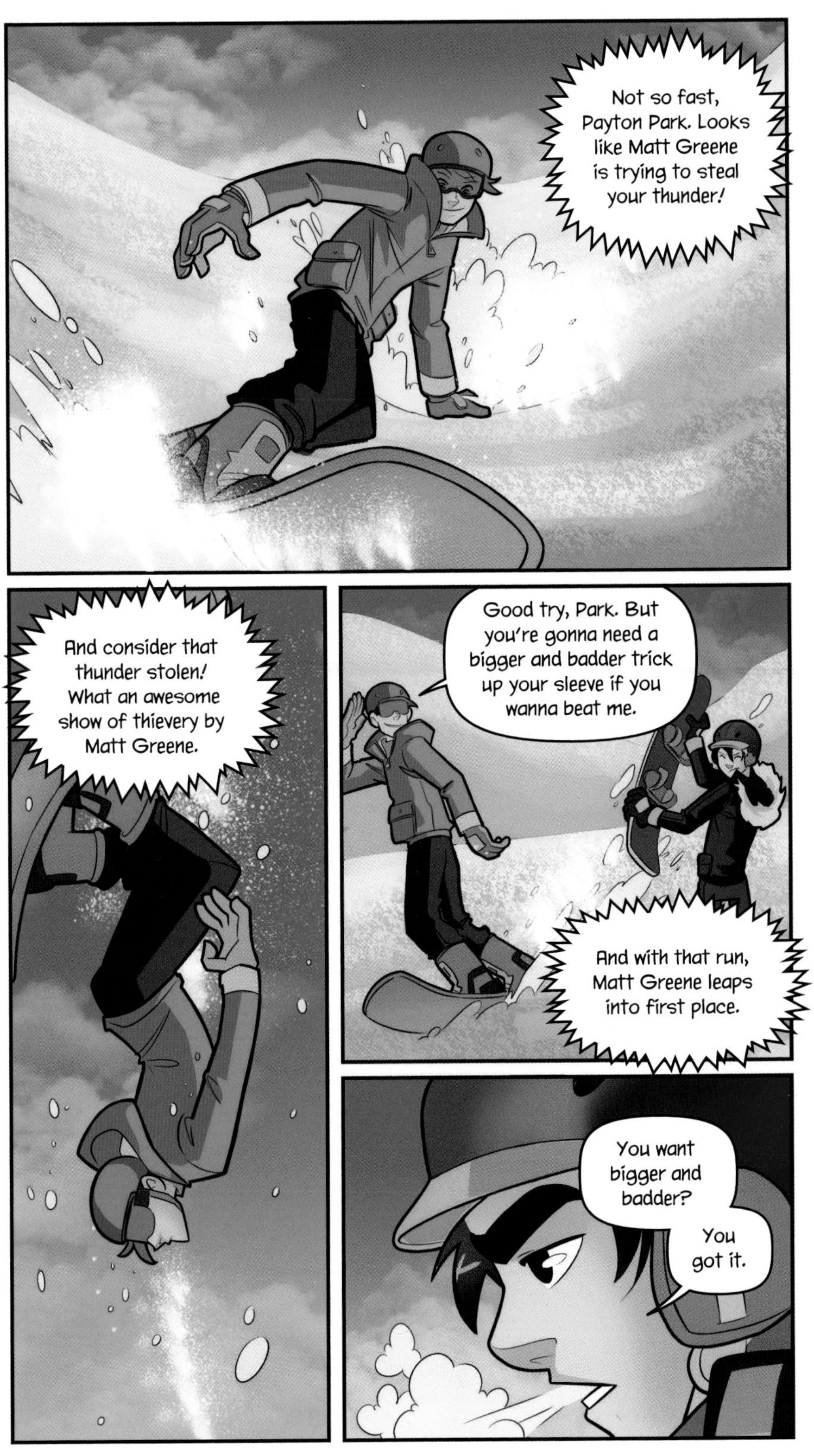
Not so fast, Payton Park. Looks like Matt Greene is trying to steal your thunder!
And consider that thunder stolen! What an awesome show of thievery by Matt Greene.
Good try, Park. But you're gonna need a bigger and badder trick up your sleeve if you wanna beat me.
And with that run, Matt Greene leaps into first place.
You want bigger and badder?
You got it.

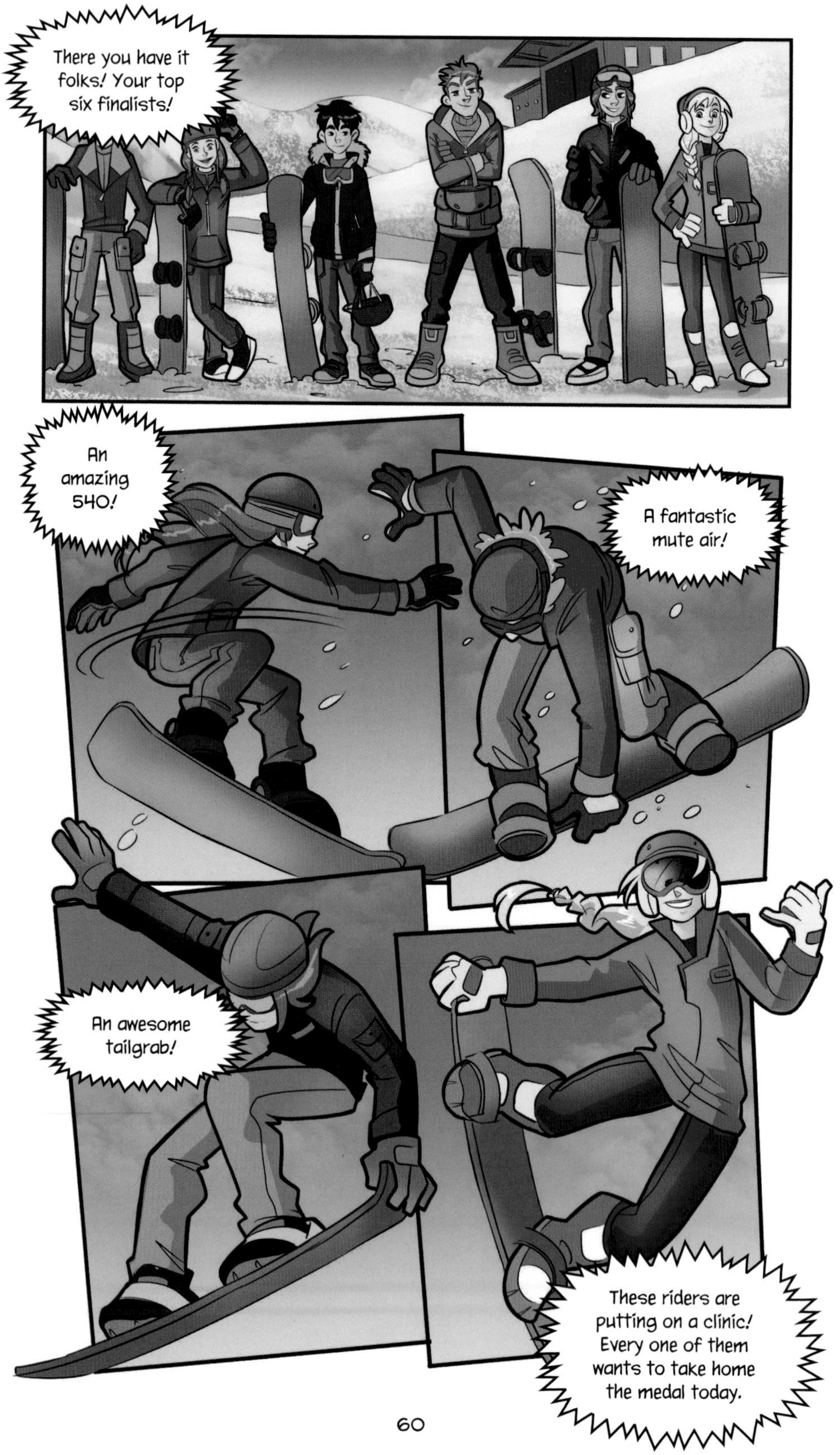
There you have it folks! Your top six finalists!
An amazing 540!
A fantastic mute air!
An awesome tailgrab!
These riders are putting on a clinic! Every one of them wants to take home the medal today.

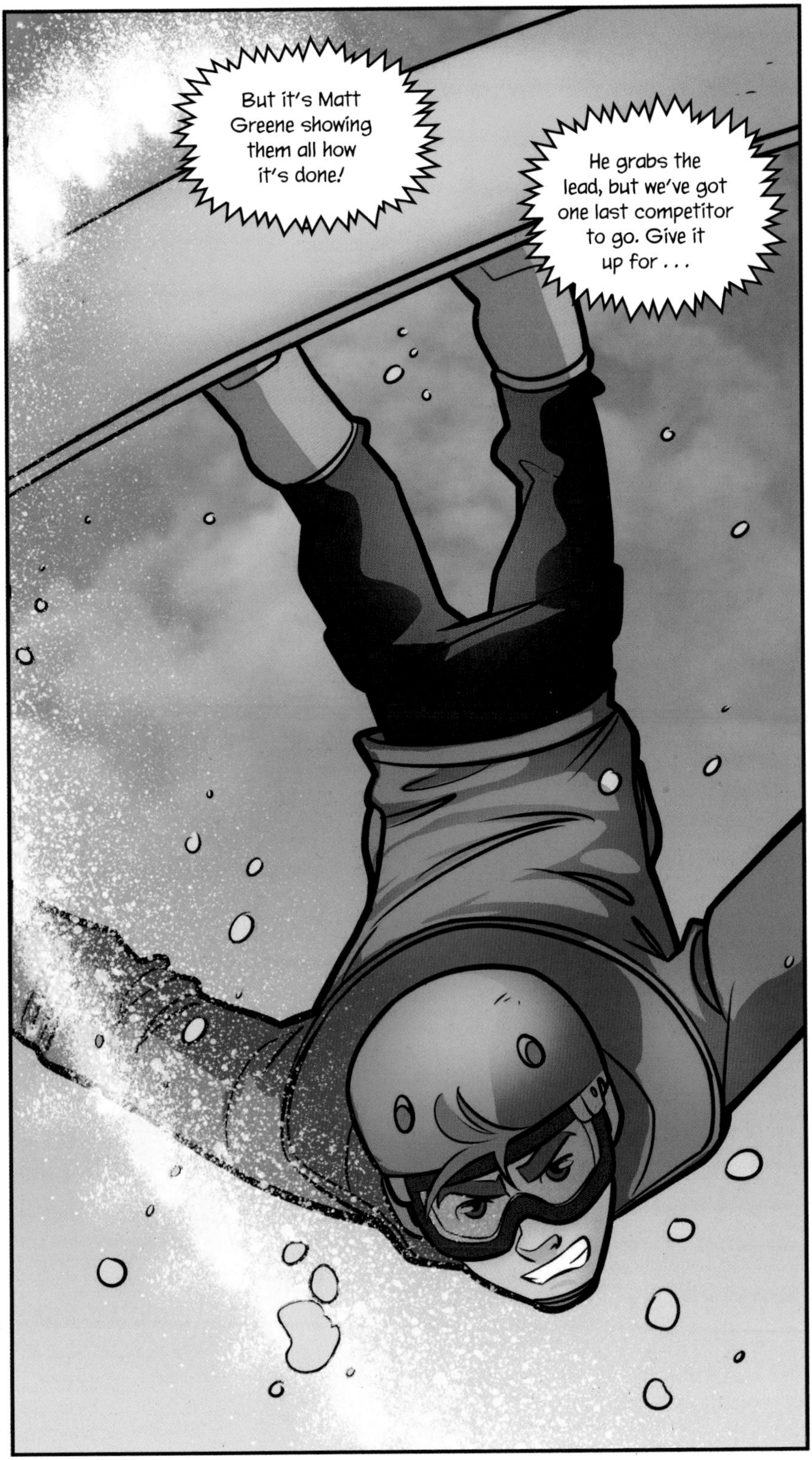
But it's Matt Greene showing them all how it's done!
He grabs the lead, but we've got one last competitor to go. Give it up for . . .

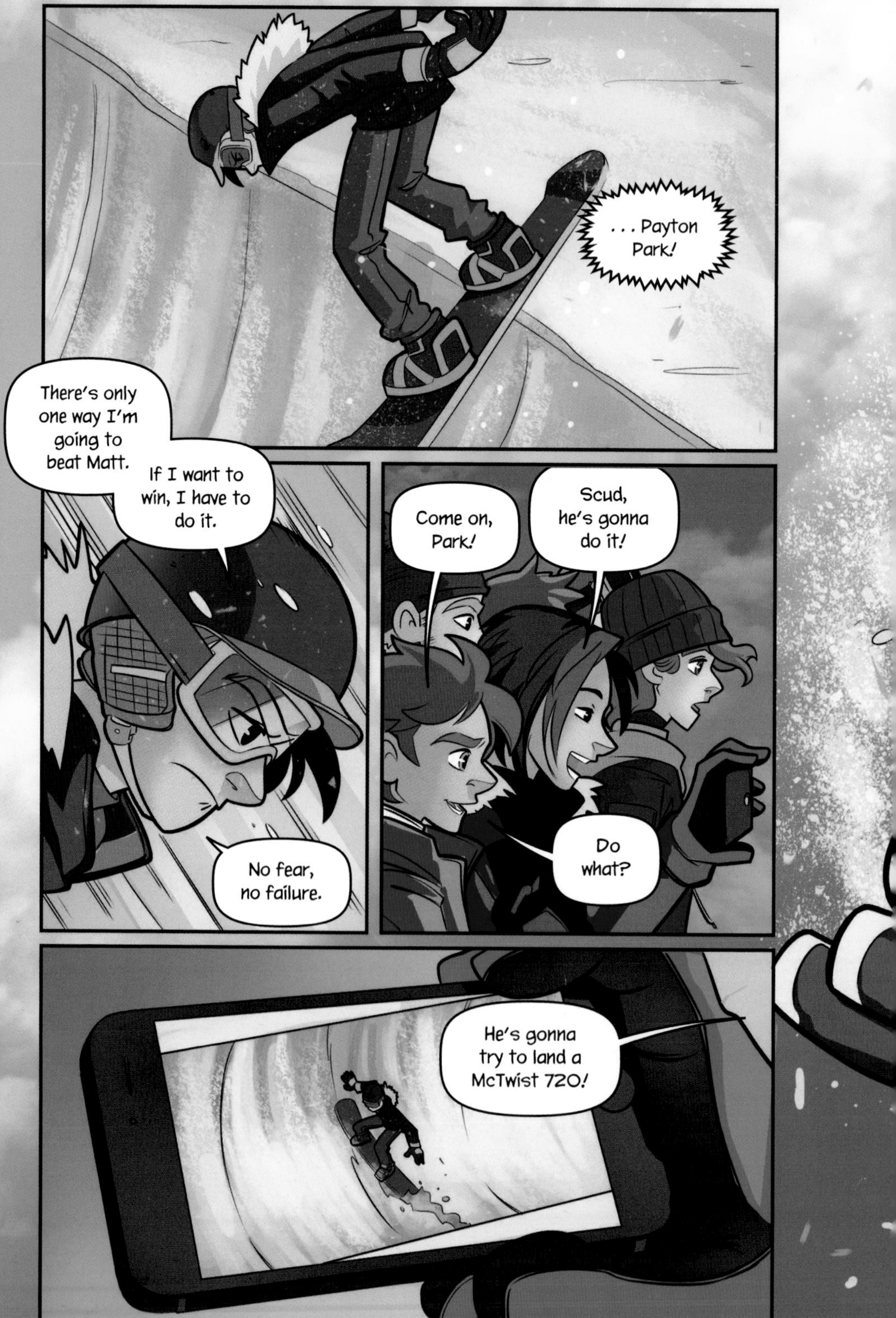
. . . Payton Park!
There's only one way I'm going to beat Matt.
If I want to win, I have to do it.
No fear, no failure.
Come on, Park!
Scud, he's gonna do it!
Do what?
He's gonna try to land a McTwist 720!

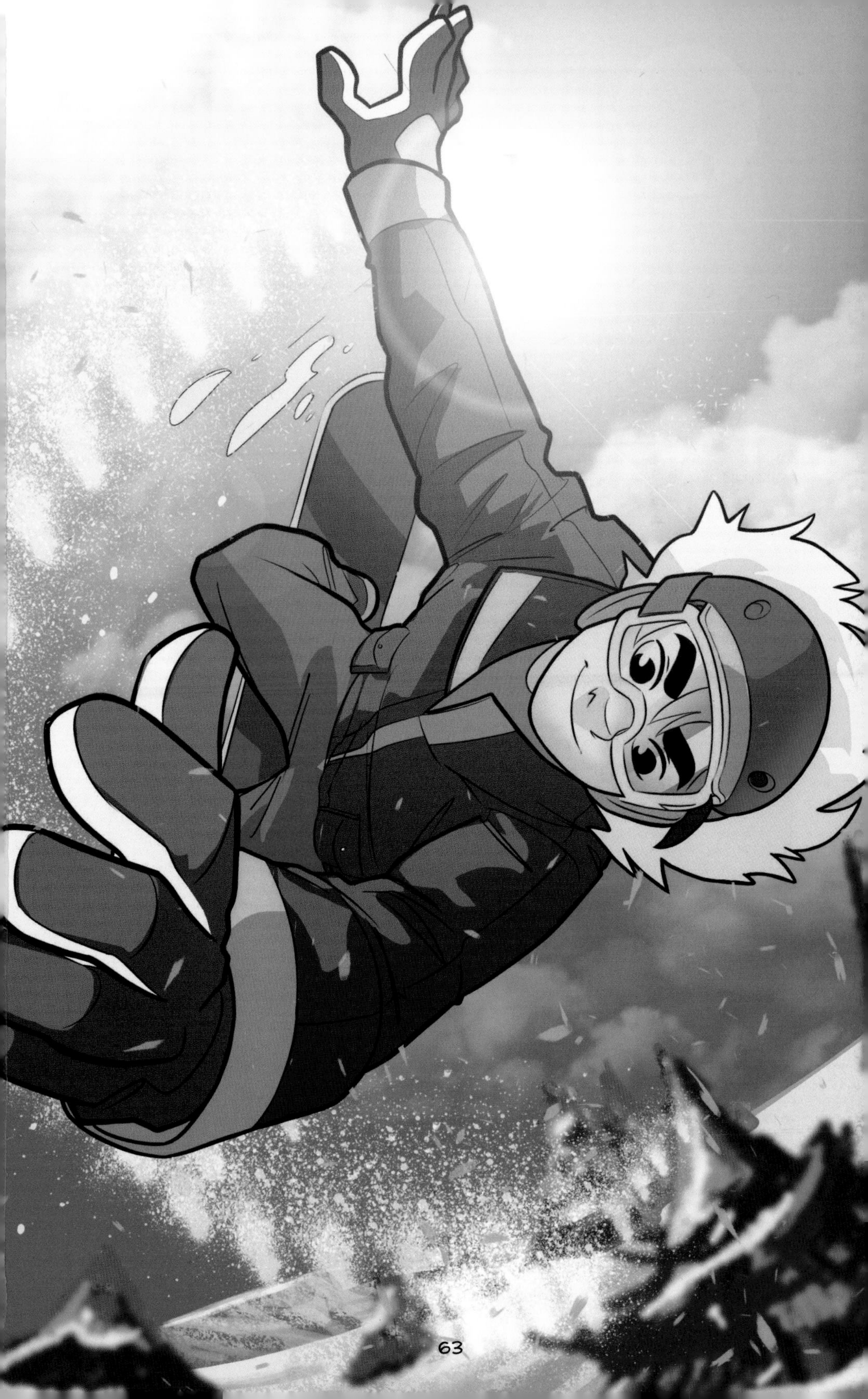

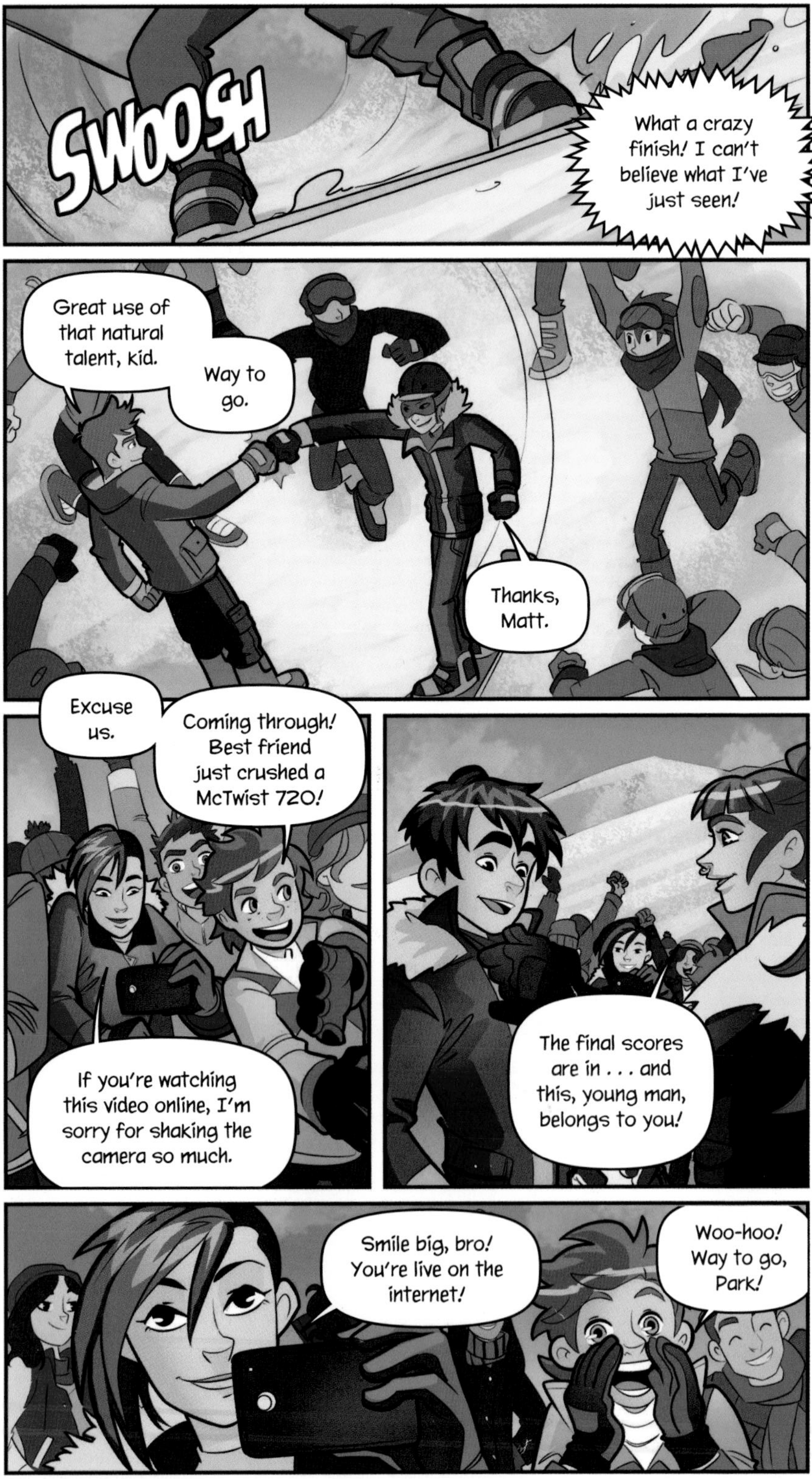

SWOOSH
What a crazy finish! I can't believe what I've just seen!
Great use of that natural talent, kid.
Way to go.
Thanks, Matt.
Excuse us.
Coming through! Best friend just crushed a McTwist 720!
If you're watching this video online, I'm sorry for shaking the camera so much.
The final scores are in . . . and this, young man, belongs to you!
Smile big, bro! You're live on the internet!
Woo-hoo! Way to go, Park!

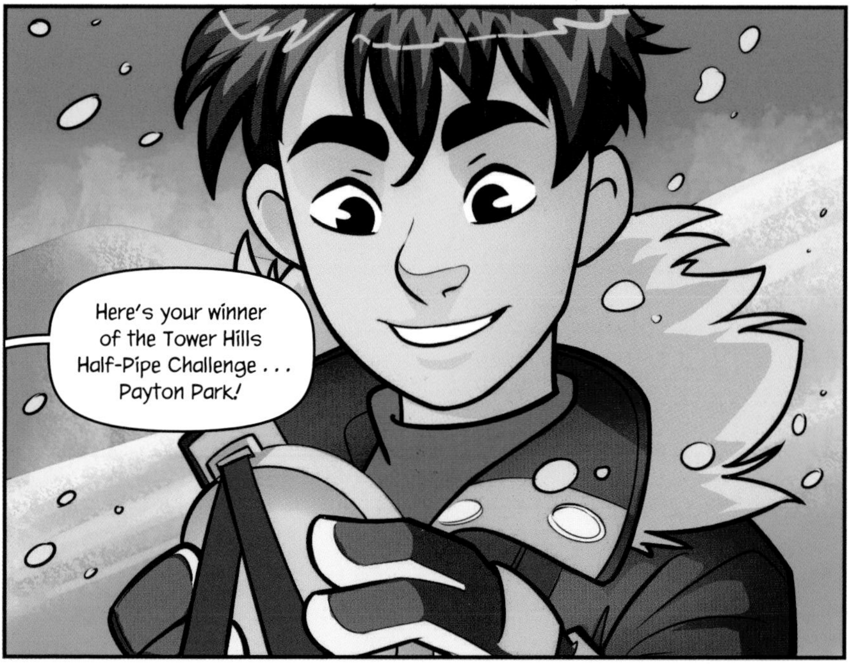
Here's your winner of the Tower Hills Half-Pipe Challenge . . . Payton Park!

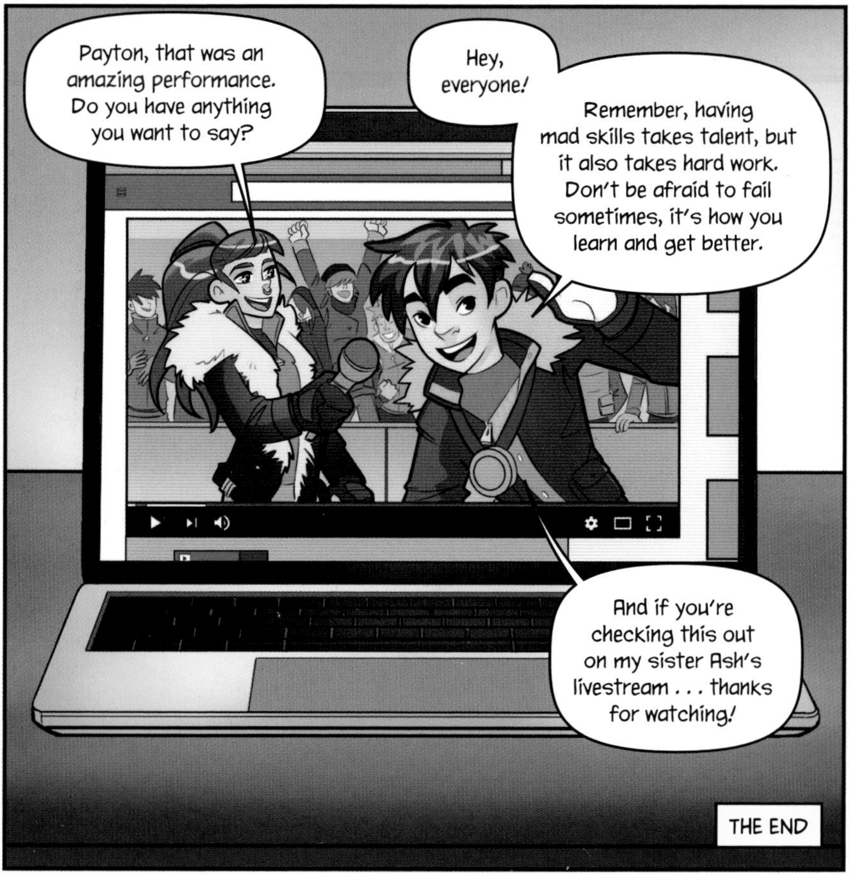
Payton, that was an amazing performance. Do you have anything you want to say?
Hey, everyone!
Remember, having mad skills takes talent, but it also takes hard work. Don't be afraid to fail sometimes, it's how you learn and get better.
And if you're checking this out on my sister Ash's livestream . . . thanks for watching!
THE END

VISUAL QUESTIONS

1. Graphic novels use art to tell a story and to show us what a character is like. The above panel shows Park in his bedroom. What can we learn about him just by studying his room?

2. Closeups are a good way to show how someone is feeling during a story. Look at the above closeup panel. How do you think the character feels in this image?

3. Artists also use dramatic angles to help tell a story. Look at the panel below and describe how you think Park is feeling at this moment.

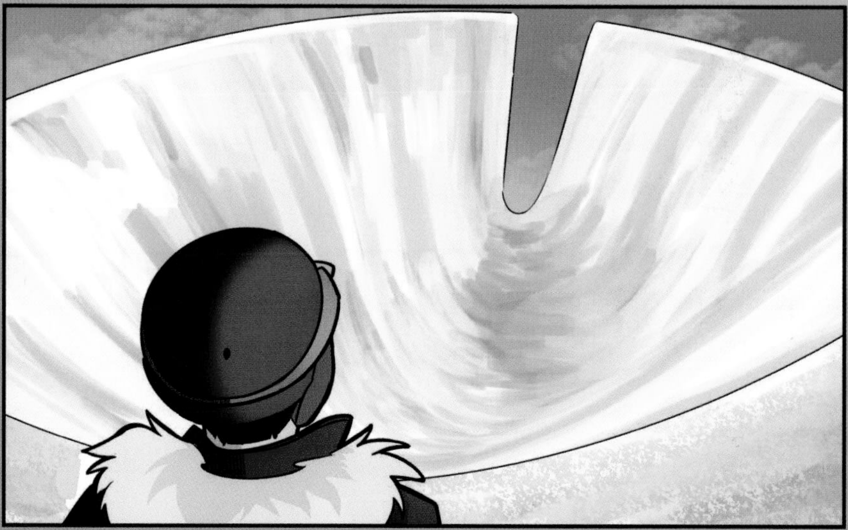

4. A series of panels can show several characters and scenes in a short amount of time to help keep the story moving. Look at the panels to the right. Can you tell what is happening in the story from the actions they show?

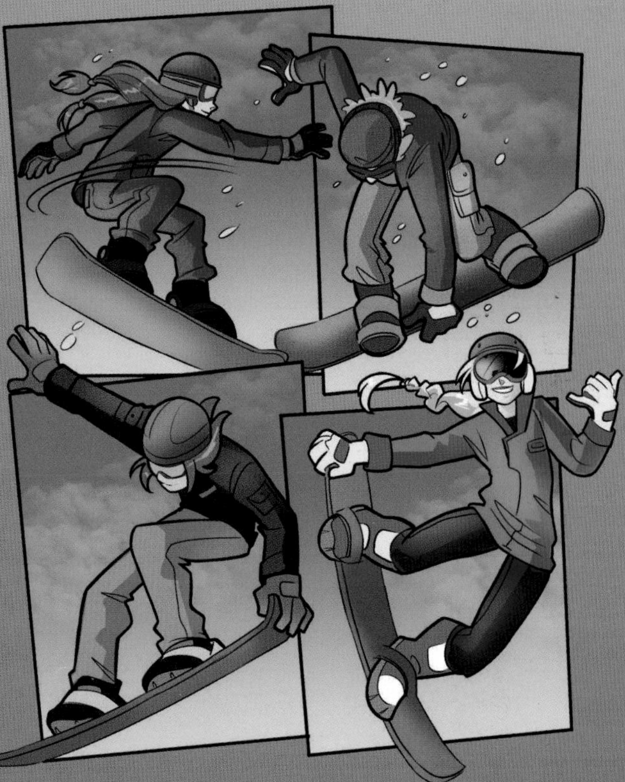

MORE ABOUT SNOWBOARDING

- Snowboarding is one of the most popular extreme sports in the world. It has been an Olympic event since 1998. The sport first debuted at the Nagano, Japan, Olympic Games that year.

- Snowboarding history is largely unknown. Many people credit M. J. Burchett from Utah with creating one of the first snowboards in 1929. He made it out of a plank of wood and used horse reins and clotheslines to secure his feet.

- The modern-day snowboard was invented in 1965 by Sherman Poppen. He wanted to create something that resembled surfing on snow. He bound two skis together into a "surf-type snow ski." Poppen originally called his device the "snurfer."

- There are several types of snowboarding events. Here are just a few:
  - In HALF-PIPE events boarders compete on a U-shaped ramp dug deep into a hill. Competitors rack up points by doing jumps, tricks, and twists.
  - SNOWBOARD CROSS is a speed competition that challenges riders to navigate through winding courses with narrow turns, jumps, berms, inclines, and drops.
  - SLOPESTYLE events are fast and wild! The courses are often covered with obstacles called "boxes" that look like big, slippery tabletops. Another obstacle often seen is the rail.

- Shaun White is one of the world's greatest boarders. He has won two Olympic gold medals in snowboarding. He's also won an amazing 24 combined medals in the Winter and Summer X Games in various snowboard and skateboard events.

SNOWBOARD TRICK GLOSSARY

360 — A trick involving one full spin while in the air.

540 — A trick involving one and one half spins while in the air.

720 — A trick involving two full spins while in the air.

BACKSIDE — When a rider spins in a clockwise direction during a trick.

FRONTSIDE — When a rider spins in a counter-clockwise direction during a trick.

METHOD AIR — A trick in which a rider bends both knees and grabs the heel edge of the board to pull it level with his or her head.

MCTWIST — A complicated trick in which a rider performs a backside 540 while doing a front flip and then lands riding forward.

MUTE AIR — A trick in which the rider grabs the toe edge of the board either between the toes or in front of the front foot.

ROCKET AIR — A trick in which the rider grabs the toe edge of the board closest to the front foot while it points toward the ground.

RODEO FLIP — A trick in which the rider performs a 540 spin while doing a frontward or backward flip at the same time.

STALEFISH — A trick in which the rider grabs the heel edge of the board between the bindings next to the rear foot.

TAILGRAB — A trick in which the rider grabs the tail end of the board while in the air.

GLOSSARY

chalet (sha-LAY)—a house or building on a mountain often used by skiers and snowboarders to rest and get warm

coping (KOH-ping)—the top edge of a half-pipe ramp

half-pipe (HAF-pipe)—a U-shaped ramp with high walls

humiliate (hyoo-MIL-ee-ate)—to make someone look or feel foolish or embarrassed

inferno (in-FUR-noh)—an intense fire

quarantine (KWOR-uhn-teen)—to keep people or animals separated to stop the spread of disease

social media (SOH-shuhl MEE-dee-uh)—forms of electronic communication, such as websites and online blogs, in which users share information, ideas, personal messages, and other content

withdraw (with-DRAW)—to remove oneself from participation in a competition

READ THEM ALL!

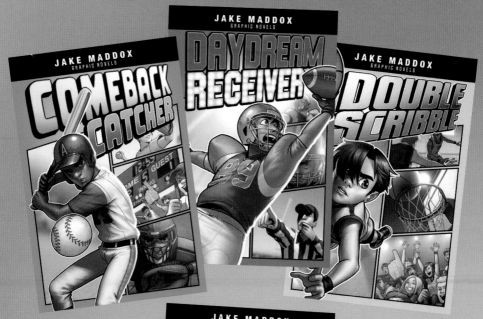

ABOUT THE AUTHOR

Brandon Terrell is the author of numerous children's books, including several volumes in both the Tony Hawk 900 Revolution series and the Tony Hawk Live2Skate series. He has also written several Spine Shivers titles, and is the author of the Sports Illustrated Kids: Time Machine Magazine series. When not hunched over his laptop, Brandon enjoys watching movies and TV, reading, watching and playing baseball, and spending time with his wife and two children at his home in Minnesota.

ABOUT THE ARTISTS

Berenice Muñiz is a Mexican artist from Monterrey. She has been drawing and coloring comics since 2009. Her work can be found on several children's books in her country, where she lives with her beloved partner in crime, a shaggy dog and four cats.

Nephtali Leal is a Mexican artist from Monterrey. His skills have helped him land work on comics, video games, animations, and production centers. Nep's a cinema enthusiast and he has worked on several areas such as VFX, FX motion graphics storyboarding, concept art, and more.

Jaymes Reed has operated the company Digital-CAPS: Comic Book Lettering since 2003. He has done lettering for many publishers, most notably and recently Avatar Press. He's also the only letterer working with Inception Strategies, an Aboriginal-Australian publisher that develops social comics with public service messages for the Australian government. Jaymes is also a 2012 and 2013 Shel Dorf Award Nominee.